"Making love have complications I'd prefer to avoid."

Astra stared at him uncomprehendingly for a moment or two, and then went pink when she thought she saw what he was getting at. "I might get pregnant?" she questioned coolly, if a touch self-consciously.

"I was thinking more that, not knowing the rules, the way these things work, you might be the clinging type," he corrected her.

"Clinging!" She was furious on the instant. "From gratitude, obviously," she hurled at him.

She saw his lips twitch. Pleasantly he enlightened her. "You might want marriage."

Marriage? Never! How dared he? "To you? Don't flatter yourself, Baxendale."

"You're too splendid for words when you're angry."

THE MARRIAGE PLEDGE

**For three cousins it has to be marriage—
pure and simple!**

Yancie, Fennia and Astra are cousins—exceedingly close
cousins, who've grown up together and shared the same
experiences. For all of them, one thing is certain—
they'll never be like their mothers, having serial,
meaningless affairs; they've pledged that, for them,
it has to be marriage or nothing!

Only, things are about to change when three eligible
bachelors walk into their lives—and each cousin finds
herself with a new boss...and a potential husband?
But will each of their stories end at the altar?
This month it's Astra's turn!

The Marriage Pledge
by Jessica Steele

HARLEQUIN ROMANCE®
3588—THE FEISTY FIANCÉE
3615—BACHELOR IN NEED
3627—MARRIAGE IN MIND

Don't miss any of our special offers. Write to us at the
following address for information on our newest releases.

Harlequin Reader Service
U.S.: 3010 Walden Ave., P.O. Box 1325, Buffalo, NY 14269
Canadian: P.O. Box 609, Fort Erie, Ont. L2A 5X3

MARRIAGE IN MIND

Jessica Steele

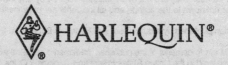

HARLEQUIN®

TORONTO • NEW YORK • LONDON
AMSTERDAM • PARIS • SYDNEY • HAMBURG
STOCKHOLM • ATHENS • TOKYO • MILAN • MADRID
PRAGUE • WARSAW • BUDAPEST • AUCKLAND

If you purchased this book without a cover you should be aware
that this book is stolen property. It was reported as "unsold and
destroyed" to the publisher, and neither the author nor the
publisher has received any payment for this "stripped book."

ISBN 0-373-03627-2

MARRIAGE IN MIND

First North American Publication 2000.

Copyright © 2000 by Jessica Steele.

All rights reserved. Except for use in any review, the reproduction or
utilization of this work in whole or in part in any form by any electronic,
mechanical or other means, now known or hereafter invented, including
xerography, photocopying and recording, or in any information storage
or retrieval system, is forbidden without the written permission of the
publisher, Harlequin Enterprises Limited, 225 Duncan Mill Road,
Don Mills, Ontario, Canada M3B 3K9.

All characters in this book have no existence outside the imagination of
the author and have no relation whatsoever to anyone bearing the same
name or names. They are not even distantly inspired by any individual
known or unknown to the author, and all incidents are pure invention.

This edition published by arrangement with Harlequin Books S.A.

® and TM are trademarks of the publisher. Trademarks indicated with
® are registered in the United States Patent and Trademark Office, the
Canadian Trade Marks Office and in other countries.

Visit us at www.eHarlequin.com

Printed in U.S.A.

CHAPTER ONE

ASTRA stared incredulously at her immediate boss. 'You're saying he wants *us,* Yarroll Finance, to work out some sort of financial package for him?' she questioned disbelievingly.

'It hasn't got that far,' Norman Davis cautioned. 'Mr Baxendale made contact this morning while you were out. Apparently word has reached him of our dynamic financial adviser, and he wants to see you.'

'Me!' she exclaimed. 'Mr Baxendale wants to see *me?*'

'You,' Norman Davis confirmed.

Astra was stunned. She knew, without false modesty, that she was good at her job. But that Sayre Baxendale, a board member of Blyth Whitaker International—and a man to be reckoned with, according to a report she had read in some financial paper only last week—should consult them was astounding. That he should approach Yarroll Finance when it came to matters of personal finance was staggering enough—and it had to be personal finance if she was involved, because that was the area in which she excelled. But that he should ask for her, in particular, to talk facts and figures with was astonishing.

'You're sure it's me he wants to see?' she questioned, her habit of double-checking everything to do with her work starting to kick in.

'If you're Miss Astra Northcott,' Norman Davis beamed. Yarroll Finance was a highly respected company; to have a director of Blyth Whitaker International on their books was yet another indication of their first-class reputation in the world of finance.

Astra stared solemnly at him. She was twenty-two and was young, she knew, to hold the position she did in a firm of such superior standing. But she had studied hard for her qualifications. Had worked hard and, given that she seemed to have a natural flair for figures and hard work, this—to be asked for personally by such an esteemed client, and client he would be if she had to work twenty-five hours a day to get him the package he wanted—seemed to her to be the very ultimate of success in the finance world.

Then she allowed herself a smile. Her lovely lips parted to reveal beautiful white, perfectly even teeth, her happiness showing in the large green depths of her beautiful eyes. 'I'd better ring him to make an appointment,' she suggested. 'Do you have his home number?'

'The appointment's already made,' her boss informed her cheerfully. 'Sayre Baxendale's a very busy man. He'll see you at his office at two-thirty tomorrow afternoon.'

Astra would have liked to have fixed a *mutually* convenient time—she knew she was scheduled to be busy elsewhere at two-thirty tomorrow, and hated breaking appointments. But he who paid the piper called the tune, and apparently what Mr Baxendale wanted Mr Baxendale got. Two-thirty tomorrow was convenient for him—end of story.

Her flicker of irritation with Sayre Baxendale at what to her seemed to be a mite high-handed had long since gone by the time she arrived home that night. She'd had a busy day, and it wasn't over yet.

She took her briefcase into her study, but before she started work again she went and took a shower, put a delicious-looking lasagne in the microwave to defrost and spent an hour unwinding from the demands of the day.

If, that was, thinking about tomorrow's appointments could be called unwinding. Thankfully, in order to accommodate Sayre Baxendale, she had been able to re-schedule tomorrow's original two-thirty appointment; things had worked out well, as it happened, because the alternative time now suited her client better.

Astra went over again all she had been able to glean that day about the man she was to see tomorrow. Though what she had found out did not amount to very much, she realised. She had known already that he was on the board of Blyth Whitaker, a company with many subsidiary companies but dealing for the most part in manufacturing industries. Today's trawl had revealed he was thirty-six—younger than she had supposed a man of his business repute to be. She had learned that, while never lacking some sensational-looking female to squire around, he was unmarried.

So what was this bachelor director, presumably without children, doing looking to Yarroll Finance for some sort of financial package? Astra stepped from her shower, donned a robe, fixed herself a salad to go with the lasagne and continued to question.

Without a doubt, Blyth Whitaker fielded their own finance department—so why was he coming to Yarroll Finance? Astra was munching her way through her meal when she settled for the only logical answer—Sayre Baxendale must want to keep his personal business separate from the company he worked for. Yes, that must be it. He wanted to keep his personal dealings totally private from his own people.

So why, if he wanted to keep it so private, had he asked that she should call and see him at his place of business? She was used to visiting clients in their own homes—she'd have thought he would have instructed that she call and see him at his home.

But perhaps he was too busy dating sensational-looking females to have any spare time! Astra grinned at the sourness of that thought—good luck to him.

She wished, though, that he had given Norman Davis

some sort of hint about what kind of package he was after. Surely it couldn't be some kind of a pension plan? Laughable! He'd have stocks and shares by the thousands, endless funds salted away to cover any eventuality; of that she was certain.

Astra liked to be well prepared before she saw any of her clients, but had just resigned herself to hoping she would have the answers to any questions Sayre Baxendale threw at her, without having to call back to base, when her telephone rang. It was her cousin, Yancie.

'I've interrupted you and you hate me?' Yancie apologised in advance.

'You didn't and I don't.'

'You're in your study.'

'I'm not—I'm in the kitchen and I've just finished eating a lasagne Fennia made some time ago.'

'Have you heard from her?'

'Not yet.'

'Neither have I—which isn't at all surprising. Now—what am I going to do about you?'

'Don't you *dare!*' Astra threatened, recalling again her horror when, at Fennia's wedding a couple of weeks ago, Yancie had said 'And then there was one' with such a meaningful gleam in her eye—Astra now the only one of the three cousins remaining unmarried. Astra had had to tell her cousin to scrap at once any embryo notion she might have of seeing to it that she met 'Mr Right'.

Yancie laughed at her fierce 'Don't you *dare*'. 'I wouldn't, love,' she promised. 'But with both Fen and me finding such utter bliss it doesn't seem right that you haven't. I know, I know,' she went on quickly before Astra could butt in, 'you're a career woman, happy as you are and absolutely, positively, have no interest in getting married. But, honestly, Astra, if it does happen, and you do fall in love, please—let it happen. Promise me!'

In Astra's view the possibility that she, like her two cousins, might fall head over heels in love was so remote as to be extinct. It was, therefore, no hardship to give Yancie the promise she wanted.

'Oh, I will,' she answered lightly, and changed the subject. 'How are things with you?' she asked. 'Don't answer—it's there in your voice. You're still on cloud nine.'

'Fly in the ointment,' Yancie confessed.

At once Astra wanted to do anything she could for her cousin. Yancie had been married to Thomson Wakefield only three months—nothing should be allowed to mar her happiness. 'Your mother?' she guessed.

'How well we all know one another!' And, to show that she wasn't too distressed, Yancie laughed. 'Mother's broken up with Henry and...'

'That didn't last long!'

'Does it ever? Anyhow, for some unknown reason, my mother wants to come and stay with me for a while.'

'Grief!' Astra exclaimed; it was relatively unheard of for any of their mothers to want very much to do with their daughters, much less ask to come and stay for a while.

'My sentiments exactly!'

'What does Thomson say?'

'He says to invite her—and he'll invite *his* mother to come at the same time. I think he's thinking that they'll both be such ghastly company for each other that neither of them will stay long.'

Astra remembered Thomson's sour-looking mother at his wedding—she had no trouble at all remembering Yancie's mother, her aunt Ursula. She, like her two sisters—Astra's mother and Fennia's mother—was completely flighty, man and money mad.

But, as irrepressible as ever, Yancie was laughing again as she stated, 'I think I might just do that.' And Astra burst out laughing too.

She was not laughing a little while later when she put down the phone. Memories were surfacing, memories which she had thought no longer haunted her, but all too plainly, and painfully, still did.

Her parents had divorced when she was three years old. Her mother, according to her aunts, had not particularly wanted a child but had conceived her as a ploy to get wealthy Carleton Northcott to marry her.

Astra's aunt Ursula and aunt Portia had seen nothing at all wrong in revealing to Astra when she had been in her early teens that their sister Imogen had declined Carleton Northcott's offer of a handsome maintenance settlement for her and the child. Instead, obviously knowing something of the integrity of the man—for all it seemed he'd balked at having to actually marry her—Imogen Jolliffe, as she was then, had horrified him by telling him it was marriage—or an abortion.

So Imogen had got what she wanted. It hadn't been enough for her. Whether the marriage would have worked had she kept to her marriage promises was difficult to tell, but her baby had been barely six months old when Mrs Carleton Northcott started playing in pastures new.

Astra remembered little of those early years. What she did remember was that, for all her father no longer lived with them, she saw more of him than she saw of her mother.

In her early years Astra grew used to being banished to her room on the occasions when her mother brought 'a friend' home. As it happened, Astra, a quiet, reserved child, was quite happy not to have to stay and be talked at by the succession of men who filed through the house.

Had she stayed at home, however, she might—while shying away from it—have formed the opinion over her growing years that her mother's promiscuity was normal behaviour. Though her father had been ready to put a stop to any chance of that.

She was just coming up to her seventh birthday and had spent a very pleasant weekend with him when, according to her aunt Delia, her mother's elder half-sister, her father had been disturbed by Astra's innocent chatter about the story book she'd been reading in her bedroom while her mother had talked to 'Uncle' William in her bedroom.

Instead of returning Astra to her home at the end of her weekend stay with him, it was to her aunt Delia's house that he took her. 'Stay here with Aunt Delia, poppet; I just want to go and have a private word with Mummy,' he explained, having had a discussion with her aunt while Astra went to chatter to Mollie, Aunt Delia's mongrel dog.

Astra loved her aunt Delia; everything was so calm around her, and with one arm around Mollie Astra waved her father off with the other. She had no inkling then of the almighty row that had taken place between her parents. Which, pieced together many years later, started with her father saying he had merely called to inform her mother personally that Astra wasn't coming back, and that he was taking her to live with him.

Apparently, for all it was plain that Imogen Northcott had little interest in her child, she cared not at all to have her ex-husband laying down the law. 'No, you are not!' Imogen told him bluntly, and in the ensuing 'Yes I am, no, you're not' argument his ex-wife informed him she had made arrangements—without consulting him—for Astra to go to boarding-school.

Carleton Northcott might have argued, but immediately saw that, while he still followed his business interests and much though he had grown to love his daughter, he would not be able to be a full-time father to her. Since his main objective was to get her from under her mother's roof— perhaps boarding-school might be the answer.

'She's only seven.' He wasn't ready to give in easily. 'She'll be lonely—I'm not having her...'

'She won't be lonely. Her two cousins are going with her.'

Cold dislike had been in the air as Carleton Northcott looked at the woman he'd been forced to marry. 'How long have you and your harpy sisters been planning this?' he had wanted to know.

Imogen had smiled a triumphant smile as she informed him, 'From the day she was born. Unfortunately, the boarding-school we've chosen wouldn't take them younger than the age of seven.'

Astra had been happy at boarding-school. All three cousins were born within a month of each other, and, rooming together as they did, Astra, Yancie and Fennia became as close as sisters. Apart from school holidays, they were inseparable.

Astra considered herself the lucky one in that both Fennia and Yancie's fathers had died, and while Astra, too, sometimes had an 'uncle' come to collect her at the end of school term more often than not it was her father who came for her.

Though, because he was busy a lot of the time, her mother demanded that she spend her school holidays at home with her. This, Astra soon discovered, was more to spite her father than from any deep-rooted maternal instinct. For Imogen, married again and now Imogen Kirby, was still carrying on as though she had never said 'I do' to Robert Kirby.

Holidays, apart from the time Astra spent at her father's smart apartment, were in the main fairly awful. She couldn't wait to get back to school—the same went for her two cousins. Astra clearly remembered how the three of them had met up again after a lengthy summer break and Yancie, having gone through a shocking time, had fervently declared, 'No, no, no, no way am I going to be like my mother.'

'That goes double for me and my mother!' Fennia, having gone through a dreadful traumatic time too, unhappily asserted.

'And that's triple for me!' Astra had chipped in, having been aghast at the way her mother had barely waited for the door to close on husband number two, whenever he left for his office, before she was on the phone to some other man.

Having spent weeks in the same close confines with their female parents, each cousin—aware enough by then, educated enough by then—had been absolutely appalled by what they had seen and heard going on. Absolutely appalled and—afraid!

'What if we've inherited something?' Fennia exclaimed, aghast. 'A gene, or something—some promiscuous part of our mothers that makes them the way they are when any likely-looking man pokes his head above the parapet!'

They had gasped in dismayed consternation—it was truly a terrifying thought. And it was there and then, after a lengthy and fearful discussion, that the cousins vowed that they would defy any such wayward gene should it rear its ugly head. They would not be permissive, promiscuous or free-moralled. They would, they pledged, be alert and ready to stamp on any wayward urge that showed itself.

There had been no need to renew that vow two years later when, at the age of eighteen, they had left boarding-school for the last time. It was by then as if written in stone. There would be no string of lovers. Only one man would do. The right man. If they didn't find him, they would give themselves to no man.

Yancie and Fennia's 'right' men had come along, and they had married them. Astra, having undergone further extensive and in-depth business training, was career-minded and dedicated to her job. She had hopes of going higher and yet higher up the professional ladder. Marriage simply had no place in her plans.

She worked hard, evenings and weekends, and had no time for any kind of a relationship. Which was fine by her—she'd seen enough of her mother's 'relationships' to know that that route wasn't for her.

Not that Astra was lacking for offers. She had rich red hair, green eyes and, though naturally pale, a dream of a perfect skin. Her figure, while slender, curved in all the right places. And, according to Sukey Lloyd—a girl the three cousins had been at school with—Astra had legs to die for.

While feeling quite friendly on the inside to her fellow man, Astra found she could do little about her cool, aloof-looking exterior. Indeed, she had been completely unaware of her cool and aloof look until a couple of months ago when she'd turned down yet another invitation out from a newcomer to Yarroll Finance, who, peeved at her crisp thank-you-but-no, went away muttering, 'Now I know why they call you North Pole Northcott!'

She hadn't thought that had bothered her but, friendly with one of the secretaries who sometimes did some work for her, Astra found herself one day asking her if everybody at Yarroll's had a nickname.

'Only the favoured few,' Cindy had replied. And, on a gasp as she realised what lay behind the question, she exclaimed, 'You've heard?'

'North Pole Northcott?'

'Oh!' Cindy murmured—and, obviously trying to make light of it, added, 'Never mind—your mum loves you.'

That, Astra considered, was extremely doubtful. She had returned to live with her mother when she had finished school, but that arrangement had never been going to work. Her mother lived an idle life of socialising and greed.

Astra—to her mother's shame—wanted to work for her living.

It was a constant bone of contention between them that Astra, while living at home, was taking a full-time course which involved taking further exams for her chosen career. So that by the time Carleton Northcott decided to retire and move to his second home in the Windward Islands, and suggested that if Astra didn't want to go to Barbados with him she could move into his London apartment and keep an eye on the place for him, Astra thought it the best idea she'd heard in a long while. Her mother must have thought so too, for this time she raised no objection.

All of which had worked out for the best, Astra reflected as she washed her used dishes at the kitchen sink. Over the last few years, what with being so busy with her job, and Imogen having a full social calendar, Astra rarely saw her mother. Though, dutifully, she would telephone and occasionally her mother—usually when she was having some kind of disaster with her current male, and both her sisters were engaged elsewhere—would pay her a visit.

Which, Astra thought, dragging her mind back to the present, her briefcase as yet still unopened in her study, wasn't getting the work done. She dried her hands, and ten minutes later she was totally absorbed in her work.

Strangely, though, after all the multitude of thoughts that had gone through her head that evening, when later she turned off her computer and went to bed it wasn't of her family that she thought. For quite some while she lay sleepless, her mind not on any member of her family, but on the tough-sounding board member of Blyth Whitaker International, a man she had yet to meet.

Next day, Astra arrived at the Blyth Whitaker building in good time. Incongruously, when she would have said she knew her business inside out, she suddenly started to feel a little nervous. What nonsense! she scoffed, but

couldn't deny that she was glad the mirror in the lift she
had been directed to showed her looking cool and immac-
ulate in her black suit and white silk shirt.

Briefcase in hand and in her smart plain black, two-and-
a-half-inch-heeled shoes, Astra stepped out of the lift determined to keep looking outwardly composed. On the face
of it, there was no reason why she should lose the tiniest
bit of composure—even if it was Mr Sayre Baxendale himself that she was there to see.

Even if it seemed too incredible to be true that Sayre
Baxendale had asked for her personally, she was good at
her job. Why did she feel the need to keep reminding herself of that? Good grief—she couldn't remember the last
time, or any time for that matter, when she'd had the jitters
about meeting a client. For heaven's sake, he was expecting
her; she wouldn't have got past Reception had that not been
so.

Astra found the door she was looking for, and, since she
was expected, tapped on it only lightly, and went in. A tall
black-haired man was at another door with a woman in her
late twenties who was on her way out so that Astra caught
only a glimpse of her. The woman seemed vaguely familiar.
But Astra met so many people in her job that it didn't
surprise her that the woman, his PA, most probably, could
be someone she had already met.

However, she was here to see Sayre Baxendale, who had
closed the door after the woman and was coming back into
his office. 'Astra Northcott, Yarroll Finance,' she introduced herself. She was softly spoken, her voice unaccented,
with a hint of friendliness—otherwise her appearance and
everything else about her was totally businesslike.

She extended her right hand—he ignored it. 'Take a
seat,' he instructed shortly.

Astra didn't know what it was about this man; he was
good-looking certainly, was broad-shouldered, without fat,

had dark eyes, and she could well imagine that sensational-looking females would come chasing after him rather than him having to exert himself. But she felt more niggled by him than anything else. No one had ever declined to shake hands with her before.

Astra was aware that his dark glance was giving her a thorough going over, as if to note every detail—her figure, her thick red hair, worn as she usually wore it in a sophisticated chignon, her green eyes, her pale skin. She felt herself dissected—and put back together again—and that too annoyed her.

Which left her, since she instantly did not care at all for this man with whom she was here to do business, to draw on every scrap of her professionalism. She went calmly over to the chair he had indicated—it was opposite to the one he took—his large, uncluttered desk in between them.

'I am unsure which kind of personal package you may be interested in, Mr Baxendale,' she remarked pleasantly, placing her briefcase on his desk. 'If you'd care to give me a few details of what you have in mind,' she went on, her long, slender fingers already at the fasteners on her briefcase, 'I'll...'

'I'm not remotely interested in any personal package you have to offer.' He cut her off before she could finish, and Astra, her fingers falling away from her briefcase, just sat and stared at him, stunned.

He'd somehow made that sound as if she wanted him to be personally interested in her! Fat chance! She started to recover from her incredulity, and almost told him that it sounded to her as if his sensational females should be less forthcoming than they were if he thought she was remotely interested in him either—personally. But she was here on business, or thought she was, and to have him, Sayre Baxendale, as one of her clients would be a prize indeed.

So she remained calm, remained even a hint friendly, as

she enquired, 'You are Sayre Baxendale? I am speaking with the same man who contacted Yarroll Finance yesterday and suggested I come to see you today?'

'I asked you to come and see me today,' he replied bluntly, no suggestion about it.

Somehow Astra managed to keep a pleasant look on her face. 'I must have got it wrong,' she murmured apologetically. 'You're more interested in some commercial...' She broke off; she saw he was looking at her sceptically. And anyhow she didn't 'do' commercial. Her intelligence going into overdrive, she had a positive notion that if his Finance section couldn't come up with everything he wanted on the commercial side, then heads in that section would roll thick and fast. 'You're neither interested in a personal package nor anything commercial, are you, Mr Baxendale?' she enquired as calmly as she could.

He studied her, his dark eyes fixing at last on her cool green ones. 'No,' he answered shortly.

Instinctively, Astra wanted to get up and walk out of there. But she was here representing her firm and, anyhow, she was more professional than that. 'May I ask, then, why you have asked to see me today?' she enquired—and very nearly dropped when he told her.

However, he did not tell her straight away, but first, to her surprise, referred her to someone she had completed a deal with several months before. 'Does the name Ronald Cummings mean anything to you?' he asked.

It was a name she was unlikely to forget! She'd had a client named Ronald Cummings. That was to say she had dealt with—long and tediously—Ronald Cummings, a fifty-year-old who'd changed his mind constantly in the months prior to him finally settling on the investment she had arranged for him.

'I'm afraid I'm not at liberty to discuss anyone who may

or may not be a client,' she kept her professional hat firmly in place to reply.

Sayre Baxendale was unimpressed. 'Ronald Cummings has no such ethics when it comes to discussing you!' he informed her shortly.

'You know Mr Cummings?' Astra enquired, more to give herself a moment to sort out in her head what the dickens was going on here than anything else.

'His daughter happens to be my PA,' Sayre Baxendale answered crisply.

'His daughter?' The woman she had caught a glimpse of just now? Astra speedily thought back to three or four months ago, grateful that she had an excellent memory. No wonder the woman looked familiar—she had met her. 'Mrs Edwards,' she pulled out of nowhere, and didn't think that was too bad considering she had met the woman only once. But this was no time for self-congratulation; Sayre Baxendale was looking every bit as tough as she'd heard he could be. 'Mrs Edwards, Mr Cummings's daughter, is your PA?' she questioned.

He didn't deign to answer. Straight-to-the-point-Baxendale, Astra dubbed him. 'We were speaking of Ronald Cummings and the extremely bad advice you gave him.'

'Bad advice!' she echoed, staring at him disbelievingly.

'Not to say bordering on the criminal,' Sayre Baxendale didn't flinch from accusing.

'Criminal!' Astra exclaimed, and as anger stormed through her at such a heinous accusation she flared hotly, 'I very much hope you can substantiate such a remark.' My stars! This man was the end! 'Neither my company nor I will put up with such defamation...'

'I'm sure Yarroll Finance will be delighted to know that their representative is far more interested in earning a fat commission than in...'

'That's *outrageous!*' Astra flew, rising furiously to her feet and glaring at the objectionable man who stared back at her, imperturbable, when she felt angry enough to hit him.

'It would be, if it were untrue,' he replied, rising to his feet and staring down at her. 'However, I've seen for myself the Porsche you drive—which takes quite a chunk out of your income in monthly repayments, I suspect...' What impertinence! The car was paid for! '...and that suit you're wearing would put most women back three months' salary.'

There was so much Astra could have said in her defence to such a charge. For one, that she had bought her car with only a *part* of an inheritance from her paternal grandfather. For another, she could have told Sayre Baxendale that her father insisted on paying considerable sums into her bank account from time to time. In fact, she could have told Baxendale that, if the truth be known, she had not the smallest need to work at all. As for the commission she'd earned on the Ronald Cummings package—and, recalling the way the man had dithered and constantly changed his mind, oh, my, how she'd earned it—commission had been the last thing on her mind throughout the whole transaction.

But she said none of those things, and indeed did not so much as attempt to defend herself. Very much to her own surprise, she had to admit, she heard herself actually bluntly enquire, 'You've seen my car?'

If he too was surprised that she chose to enquire rather than defend, he didn't show it, but told her equally bluntly, 'Veronica Edwards drew my attention to you getting out of your car the other day when we were in Great Portland Street on business.' That was a week ago! Astra recalled she had been in Great Portland Street a week ago. 'Where I saw you and your car is incidental,' Sayre Baxendale stated, clearly not prepared to waste any more of his precious time. 'I've seen all the papers relative to the deal you put together for Ronald Cummings; the near criminal investment you calculated for him—forgetting completely to mention that he stood to lose his home, his property if he...'

'I would have told him that!' Astra exclaimed hotly—it would have been second nature to do so. 'I...'

'Where?' Baxendale demanded. 'It's not written anywhere!'

Wasn't it? She couldn't remember. 'You have the advantage over me, you've seen the paperwork recently. I'll have to check...'

'And when you do check also that there wasn't a better deal you could have sold him.'

How dared he? Putting financial deals together was her job! What did he know about it? 'You're saying you know that there is?' she challenged, angry sparks flashing in her wide green eyes.

Sayre Baxendale stared at her for long moments before he crisply replied. 'I wouldn't presume to know anything of the sort.' Though, before she could take any comfort from that, he was going on toughly, 'According to my finance people, not only have you advised this man extremely badly, you have also overlooked the fact that, though not yielding such a handsome commission, but bearing in mind the full knowledge you have of the man and his circumstances, there was a much more suitable package you could have sold him.'

Astra stared at him in disbelief, that offensive 'handsome commission' remark barely touching her. Without question, Baxendale's finance people would be on top of the job, but... 'I doubt very much that your finance section have all the details,' she defended bravely—of course they had all the details; Veronica Edwards was the man's daughter; she'd have shown them completely everything. 'But I'll check it out.'

'Good!' Baxendale retorted. 'And when you've checked

perhaps you'll come back and tell me what you intend to do about it.'

Astra read three distinct messages in that last sentence. One, she had just been dismissed from this interview. Two, this man was convinced that he was right and that she was wrong. Three—and there was a threat there—that if she didn't check it out he would be on to her employers, the highly respected Yarroll Finance Company, *tout de suite*.

To that, Astra added a fourth. She did not take kindly to being threatened. Nor did she take kindly to the way this man had spoken to her. Never had any man spoken to her the way Baxendale had. Her pride was up in arms. My word, had she been right to wonder why he had asked to see her in connection with some private finance—all too clearly, that had never been his intention!

She stared once more into those dark, dissecting eyes, and tilted her chin a proud fraction. Then, without saying another word, she caught hold of her briefcase and headed to the door. Four—if that swine of a man was waiting for her to come back and report to him, would he have one hell of a long wait. She hoped he held his breath!

CHAPTER TWO

ASTRA'S anger against Sayre Baxendale was still on the boil when she reached her office. Oh, how she was going to enjoy sending him the sweetest of business letters telling him how she had re-checked on what was suited to Mr Cummings's circumstances at the time of their negotiations, but she could only confirm that her advice to her client had been first-class. If Mr Baxendale would care to check himself, or perhaps get his finance people to do so—she liked that line; it suggested, politely of course, that Baxendale was brain-dead in the figure department—they would see that Mr Cummings could not have been better advised. So put that in your trumpet and blow it!

She realised she would have to itemise certain details of Ronald Cummings's current finances, and to include such confidential matter went against all her instincts. But, since the man's daughter had obviously already fully discussed her father's financial standing with Sayre Baxendale and his finance department, she didn't think it could be termed as breaking client confidentiality.

Nothing if not thorough, Astra found the Ronald Cummings file on her computer, did a cursory scan and then printed out everything she had. That done, she surrounded herself with facts, figures and details of any scheme that might be even vaguely relevant to her client's circumstances. She then went back to her very first note in her dealings with him. From there, methodically, she carefully worked her way through page by page, note by note.

It had not been one of her easiest of negotiations. The man had dithered, changed his mind a number of times.

She had a note to say she had suggested to him that perhaps he might like to leave it for a short time while he thought over the several options she had suggested.

She also had a note to say no, he was adamant, he would be fifty-one in November, he thought he'd better get something arranged now. She had, in fact, she saw, many notes about what had taken place between her and her client.

Her first shock in making her in-depth scrutiny of what had taken place, however, was to find that, while she was absolutely positive she must have told Ronald Cummings that if he continued on the plan he had chosen his property might be at risk, she hadn't made a note of it. Nowhere could she find in the many letters she had written to him any note of that most important warning.

Astra's second shock came when she started fitting Ronald Cummings's details to all of the plans available at that time. Though, initially, it had seemed that nothing fitted his circumstances, in actual fact there was something that did. It was then, with thundering disbelief, she realised that, yes, there *was* a much better package she could have put to him! A package that would have been much more beneficial to him.

It was a staggering shock, and at first Astra just couldn't believe she had overlooked the much better plan. But—she had!

Because she just couldn't believe it—she was usually so methodical, so on top of her job—she double- and triple-checked out every fine detail. But, galling though it was, Sayre Baxendale had been right! In the light of this other plan, her client had been very badly advised! How could she have made such a dreadful mistake? Normally she was so clear-headed.

Astra thought back to the time when her negotiations with Ronald Cummings had started to take shape. And then she realised how her normal diligence with regard to her work must have slipped. It had been around that time that her much loved cousin Yancie had been involved in a car accident. Yancie hadn't been seriously hurt, but neither Astra nor Astra's equally much loved cousin Fennia had known that when they'd dropped everything and in a terrified panic had raced to the hospital.

They had barely recovered from that fright when Yancie had announced that she was getting married and, because neither she nor Thomson had wanted to wait very long, her two intended bridesmaids had to drop everything and help her out! What with having to take time off for rushed dress fittings and everything else, Astra now realised that for the first time ever she hadn't given full attention to her job.

It was no good blaming it on the excitement of Yancie getting married, or, Astra realised, to make the excuse that surely she was entitled to a little time off. There was no excuse. Nor could she use the excuse that Ronald Cummings had changed his mind so many times, there was every probability that she had put forward the better proposal but that he had rejected it—she didn't have a note of it. And anyhow having clients who were unsure what they really wanted was all part and parcel of the job. It was *her* job to help, to advise—and she had fallen down very, very badly.

Astra took a deep breath, and, the facts staring her in the face, she accepted what she had to do. She picked up the phone and rang Norman Davis's extension. 'Is it convenient to see you straight away?' she enquired.

'Rather!' he answered jovially—and to Astra it seemed as if her boss had been sitting there just waiting for her to get in touch to tell him how her meeting with Sayre Baxendale had gone.

Armed with a sheaf of papers, Astra left her desk knowing that she was going to have to own up to negligence.

There were thousands of pounds at stake here—it was up to her to put it right.

Norman Davis was on his feet when she went into his office, a beaming smile on his face. He was not smiling ten minutes later.

There was a lot he could have said, but, although he seemed as shaken as she felt when Astra had told him everything, all he did say—and she silently thanked him for it—was, as she had supposed, 'Leave everything with me, Astra—I'll double check it all myself. But if there has definitely been a mistake it will have to be put right. Perhaps you'll come and see me in the morning.'

She left him and went straight home. That evening, knowing she had no alternative, Astra wrote out her resignation. She did not sleep well but even when she had so much else to think about one tall, black-haired, dark-eyed man whom she had met that day—and oh, she so earnestly wished she hadn't—seemed to return to her mind again and again. Oh, clear off, she fumed, punching her pillow; but for him and his interference, she might have got a decent night's sleep. Well, one thing was for sure—she was glad she was never going to have to see Sayre Baxendale again!

Astra still felt very much shaken by what had happened when she presented herself at Norman Davis's office in the morning. He was not a happy being, she could tell; she knew the feeling. Clearly his checks had shown the same results as hers—she had fallen down extremely badly on the job.

Before she handed him her resignation, however, Astra informed him that she personally would make financial reparation to their client—only for her offer to be refused. 'Yarroll Finance will take care of that,' Norman Davis insisted, letting her know, if she didn't already, how worthy the company was of its highly esteemed reputation. She had sold the plan in the company's name; the company would, therefore, take care of compensation.

There seemed nothing else to do but to hand him her resignation. Norman Davis didn't look any happier but, as she had seen no alternative but to resign, she knew he had no alternative but to accept her resignation.

'I can't tell you how sorry I am.' He took the words she had been going to say out of her mouth. 'Your work until now has been exemplary. You were tipped for much higher things.'

'I'm sorry I let you down,' Astra answered quietly, this, the whole nightmare of it, a bitter pill to swallow. They shook hands and he walked to the door with her. 'Will you write to Mr Baxendale?' she felt honour-bound to ask— she didn't want to have to do it, yet, for the sake of the company, it couldn't be ignored.

'I'll clear up the Cummings end first, then drop him a line thanking him for his interest and letting him know the matter has been settled to Mr Cummings's satisfaction,' he answered, and warmed her down-on-the-floor feeling by giving her arm an affectionate fatherly squeeze before letting her go.

Norman Davis had let her off working out her notice, so Astra went home and tried to put it all behind her. It was not that easy. Apart from the humiliation of having to resign, she was used to hard work, enjoyed hard work, and without it she felt bereft. She couldn't settle to do anything. To pick up a book and try to bury herself in its pages was beyond her.

She thought of phoning Yancie, but her cousin would be upset for her and, given that it looked as if Yancie was going to be visited by a coven of mothers, Astra didn't want her newly-returned-from-honeymoon cousin to be upset on her behalf. Her other close confidante, Fennia, was still on her honeymoon.

When Astra's inner disquiet got too much for her, she telephoned her father in Barbados. 'How's my best dad?' she asked him brightly.

'Wanting to see his best daughter,' he answered his only child. 'When are you coming to see me? You can't work all the time, you know, sweetheart.'

'As a matter of fact...'

Her phone call to her father lasted about twenty minutes. As a parent he wanted to slay all her dragons. As a former businessman of high integrity, he appreciated that Yarroll Finance had taken the only course they could: to indemnify their client, and to accept her resignation.

Astra went to bed that night trying to pin her thoughts on something other than the ghastly happenings since she had yesterday walked into Sayre Baxendale's office, introduced herself and held out her hand.

She now knew why he had refused to shake hands with her—oh, didn't she just! He'd made no bones about stating he thought she was more interested in her fat commission and it was hard luck for any poor sucker of a client who came into her orbit. Sayre Baxendale...

Oh, get out of my head, do, Baxendale. Now, should she go and stay with her father for a while—if he had his way she would go and live with him—or should she look around for another job?

She felt very pulled towards going to visit her father, but felt too restless to lounge around in Barbados doing nothing. Yet she shied away from the idea of looking for another job—should indeed any firm in the same line of business want to employ her after this!

Fortunately she was in a position where she didn't have to work. But the loss of the job she had loved and had strived so tirelessly to be perfect at was too new for her to be able to contemplate working in any other field, just yet.

Her feeling of being bereft was still with her the next

morning. It seemed odd not to have to go along to the study and make a few business phone calls. She decided to pay her mother's half-sister a visit.

'Well, look who's here!' her aunt Delia exclaimed delightedly.

'You're not going out? I should have phoned.'

'No, you shouldn't. You know I'm always pleased to see you. You're usually much too busy in that career of...' She broke off. 'Something's happened, hasn't it?'

'You always did know the three of us better than most.'

'I've always been glad the three of you have felt able to come to me when something has troubled you,' she answered.

Shrewd, lovely aunt. Astra realised her aunt had seen beneath her smile and light-heartedness, had seen that something was troubling her. 'I've resigned from my job,' Astra owned.

'Oh, my dear! You love—loved—that job so much! What on earth happened to make you do such a thing?'

It was not very pleasant to have to confess to her nearest and dearest that she hadn't had the luxury of an option but to resign. But, simply because her aunt Delia was so near and dear to her, to evade or lie to her was out of the question. So she gave her aunt a brief outline of what had happened.

'You're every inch your father,' her aunt replied after a moment. Astra had been guarding for years against any sign that she might be like her mother, so was very much cheered by her aunt's opinion. But, ignoring that Astra hadn't had much choice but to resign, Delia Alford was going on, 'Your mother would never in this world have acted so honourably. Though, come to think of it,' she smiled, 'it would never have occurred to her to get herself a job in the first place.'

Astra felt much better for her visit to her aunt Delia, but

as the weekend came and went time started to hang very heavily on her hands.

Her cousin Yancie phoned her on Tuesday with the dreaded news that the two mothers-in-law were coming to stay. 'You wouldn't care to pull the plug on that computer and come to dinner on Saturday, would you?'

Confession time. 'Er—there's no computer plug to pull,' Astra answered lightly. And, in the same light vein, she explained that she no longer had a job.

'I'm on my way!' Yancie said at once.

'No, you're not.'

'You lived and breathed that job—something must have happened. I'll come over.'

'There's no need.'

'You're upset.'

'I'll be more upset if you take time out from whatever it is you're doing to come and hold my hand. Besides, I'll be seeing you on Saturday evening,' Astra replied.

'I'll…' Yancie broke off. 'You'll come on Saturday and help take the pressure off?' she exclaimed.

'Would I let you down?'

They chatted on for ages, but Astra was remembering she had said, 'Would I let you down?' to Yancie when the very next day her half cousin, Greville, rang.

'I've just been paying a visit to my mother,' he opened. Ah! 'Aunt Delia told you?'

'If you're looking for a career in finance, I'm sure Addison Kirk would love to have you on their payroll,' Greville, a director of that firm, answered.

'The last time you got one of your cousins a job, she ended up marrying the boss!' Astra joked, never more happy for Yancie, but marriage was not a road she wanted to tread.

'Still a fate worse than death?' Greville enquired.

'That makes two of us,' she answered lightly. Greville,

tall, good-looking, his fortieth birthday imminent, had been married once some years ago, but the marriage had ended in divorce, leaving her half cousin so badly scarred that he, like Astra, avoided entanglements like the plague.

Or so she had thought, and owned she was quite surprised when he seemed to hesitate, and then said, 'Er...'

Astra knew him. She loved him. And suddenly she was remembering a remark her cousin Fennia had made shortly before her marriage to Jegar Urquart. It was something to the effect that Fennia thought that Greville was over his marriage break-up and all the pain that had gone with it.

'What gives, Greville Alford?' Astra probed gently.

'You always were smart,' he answered—and Astra waited. 'Well, since you're no longer working all hours...' He broke off—and only then, what with Yancie suggesting she worked all hours, and Greville openly saying so, did Astra realise just how glued to the grindstone she had truly been. 'The truth is, Astra, love,' he went on, 'your big cousin needs your support.'

'You've got it!' Astra told him unconditionally. Greville had always been more of a big brother to her than a cousin. She loved him dearly; all three cousins did.

'The thing is, Astra—um—I'm in something of an emotional turmoil.'

His confession jolted her. 'You?' she questioned.

'I know. Who'd have thought it?'

'You're—er—you've fallen for someone? I'm sorry,' she apologised instantly. 'I didn't mean to pry.' And, the practical side of her waking up, she rose over her shock that it looked as if her confirmed, 'never again' half cousin had fallen for someone and was 'all over the place' emotionally about it. 'How can I help?' she asked, ready, willing, eager to help him if she could. 'What do you want me to do?'

'Nothing too terrible,' he replied, and explained, 'I've been invited to this party and I happen to know that the someone I'm particularly—um—interested in will be there. And, daft though it may seem for a man of my age, I'm scared stiff I'll frighten her off if I act too eager.'

'You want me to come with you in order to keep you in check?' Astra queried, only just managing to hide her surprise—her cousin had got it badly!

'More to see that I don't make too much of a fool of myself,' he admitted, and Astra wanted to give him a hug.

He had asked for her support—she gave it unreservedly. 'I'd love to come to a party with you,' she answered cheerfully.

'Wonderful!' he cried, and sounded so like a young, enthusiastic boy that Astra had to smile. Her smile rapidly faded, though, when he went on, 'We don't want to get there too early—it'll go on all hours anyway. I'll pick you up at—say, eight-thirty—nineish, on Saturday.'

'This Saturday?' Astra queried, playing for time, her thoughts rapid. Yancie was relying on her to help keep the peace between a brace of warring mothers. Astra recalled her reply to Yancie: 'Would I let you down?'. And truly she couldn't let her down. But Greville had never let any of them down ever, and here was her chance to do something for him.

'Is this Saturday a problem, Astra?' Already Greville was starting to sound a touch disappointed.

'Nothing we can't solve between us,' Astra answered brightly, going hurriedly on, 'I've already arranged to have dinner on Saturday—with a friend. You said this party will go on all hours. Can you cope if I don't actually come with you, but come on later?'

Clearly this party on Saturday was important to her half cousin. 'Say where you'll be and I'll come and pick you up,' he at once volunteered, so eager, it seemed, to have her there to support him that there was no way he wanted to withdraw his invitation.

But Astra knew in advance that if she told Yancie that Greville was calling for her, and so much as hinted at the emotional turmoil he was in, Yancie would want to do all she could to help Greville too, and would tell her to forget about dining with them. And knowing what a barbed tongue Aunt Ursula, Yancie's mother, had when the mood was on her, Astra felt she must support Yancie too.

'That would make it too complicated with cars,' Astra smiled. 'I'll be driving myself to meet my friend,' she added, and knew Greville had seen the sense of this when he told her the name of the party givers, and their address.

'I'll leave arriving as late as I can myself,' Greville decided. 'But if you can get there as soon as *you* can,' he added, and rang off, and Astra started to realise just how seriously his emotions had been put in turmoil.

He was nervous, and jittery, and all too plainly all at sixes and sevens over this new woman in his life. And that could only mean that he had no idea how the lady felt about him. Otherwise, why would he need his half cousin along to support him? Poor darling Greville; never had she known him be anything but supremely confident. But he shouldn't worry. To know Greville was to love him.

Saturday dragged around very slowly. She had thought a deal about Greville and also about Yancie and how she deserved her happiness. And then Astra thought of Sayre Baxendale—and found it extremely annoying that he should pop into her thoughts so constantly. The reason for that, though, was plain enough. It was because of him, and his interference, that she'd had to give up her job.

To be painfully honest, she admitted, the fault was hers. And, having inherited her father's integrity, Astra felt relieved on the one hand that her oversight had come to light and that things had been put right for Mr Cummings. But that still didn't make her feel any the warmer towards Baxendale. Had Mr Cummings or his daughter contacted her, and requested her to check the investment deal, then Astra knew she would have checked her work just as thoroughly—and would have just the same brought her mistake to Norman Davis's attention. So there had been no need for Baxendale to poke his nose in. And anyway, she'd have thought he had better things to do. She was doubly glad she'd never have to see him again.

Dinner at Yancie and Thomson's home went much better than Astra had expected. The two mothers had little to say to each other, which perhaps was just as well because Astra had been brought up knowing the cutting edge of her aunt Ursula's tongue, and Thomson's mother didn't look as if she would take any prisoners. But it warmed Astra's heart to see the way Thomson's eyes followed Yancie when she crossed the room, the way his mouth curved when he heard her laugh. Purely and simply, he delighted in her.

At around ten-thirty Mrs Wakefield senior made noises about going to bed, and Astra said she must be off. 'Can't we persuade you to stay a little while longer?' Thomson enquired charmingly.

But he accepted pleasantly when she said she'd had a lovely evening, but really felt she must go. She made her goodbyes, and both Thomson and Yancie came out to her car with her.

'You're all right, Astra? You're not fretting about...'

'Of course I'm all right,' Astra laughed, and added, immediately on her cousin's wavelength, 'I'm having a wonderful rest while I decide what I'd like to do.'

'I'm sure you won't need my help,' Thomson inserted, 'but you'd be an asset to my company if you're interested in career advancement with Addison Kirk,' its chairman offered.

Yancie beamed, and Astra felt touched and, her cool and aloof image having no place in family, she kissed them both. She drove off, catching sight of them in her rear-view mirror, arms around each other, strolling back to the house. She drove to the party in the most contented frame of mind she had been in all week. It was not to last.

Astra found the house she was looking for without any trouble, and parked the Porsche in about the only place available. The house was large, the cars in the drive many. It was, she guessed, a big party. And well under way.

She rang the doorbell. A good-looking man opened the door. He was not her host, however, but someone merely passing when the bell had sounded.

He seemed much cheered to see her. 'I was thinking of going home, but things are looking up,' he leered. Spare me! Astra gave him a look that should have told him 'Don't let me stop you' but he was not to be put off. 'Leigh Jenkins,' he introduced himself, his eyes making a meal of her trim shape in her black velvet trousers and black lace top.

'Hello,' she answered coolly, and walked past him to where, through wide open double doors, she could see the party was in full swing.

She stood just inside the entrance of the crowded room. But before she could do more than look to her left Greville was there. 'I've been keeping an eye open for you,' he beamed, and as always gave her a hug and a kiss.

Astra was still in his cousinly arms, in fact, when she had a strange sensation that someone was watching her. She looked to the right—and just couldn't believe it! She *was* being watched! And her heart seemed to turn over. So much for thinking she would never see Baxendale again! There he was, tall, sardonic, those dark eyes inscrutable, looking unblinking at her.

She tilted her chin—and looked through him. He was close enough for her to see that he didn't care very much for that. Good! She couldn't have been more pleased, and pulled out of her cousin's hug to smile up at him and ask, 'How's it going?'

He bent to whisper in her ear, 'She's here; I'll introduce you.'

Over the next hour Greville introduced her to many people, though since he was being careful nothing should betray his most private of emotions at the end of that hour Astra had not the smallest notion as to which of the affable women he had introduced her to was *the* one.

Thankfully, he either did not know Sayre Baxendale or *that man* was not in the vicinity. But Greville did not get around to introducing Baxendale, anyhow. Though while she would have welcomed refusing to shake his hand had she had the chance she had no wish to embarrass her cousin. Greville and the family knew some of the details of the mistake she had made that had caused her to resign, but for reasons of confidentiality she had not mentioned any names.

Greville had no idea that she would rather spit in Sayre Baxendale's eye than say 'How d'you do' nicely to him. Though that probably went for Baxendale, as well. He'd probably cut her dead *regardless* of embarrassing anyone, should Greville attempt any such introduction. She was definitely *persona non grata*.

That thought made her angry. Not that she wanted the scurvy knave to speak to her. But her mistake had been a genuine one, and once she had known of it she had swiftly taken steps to put it right. So why was she getting upset that Baxendale thought her more interested in her commission than in her client?

Ridiculous—she wasn't upset, though she had to own that the party had started to pall. 'Um, do you want me to stay to the end?' she asked Greville.

'Had enough?'

She felt mean. She was here to support Greville. What she wanted didn't come into it. 'Not at all,' she smiled.

'I'll come too. We'll just say goodbye to our hosts,' he decided.

'No, Greville!' she protested. 'We'll stay and...'

'We'll go—and you've been a real pal.'

'I'm dying to know which one?' she stretched up to whisper in his ear.

He laughed delightedly. 'You couldn't tell? Didn't see? Couldn't guess?'

'Not by word or look,' she confirmed.

'Whew! That's a relief!' Their heads were bent in close conversation. 'I feel so—all melty inside whenever I look at her. I felt sure it would show.'

'You must have learned to keep your expression deadpan in the boardroom.' Astra might have added more, only just then she happened to glance across the room—and caught Sayre Baxendale's dark-eyed, hostile gaze head-on.

Words died on her lips, but even as she adopted a cool pose and looked elsewhere she seemed powerless to be aware of anything but him. And then Greville was saying firmly, 'Come on, sweetheart, let's find our hosts.'

By the time they had thanked their hosts and said a few goodbyes they were leaving the room, and Astra was relegating to the bin any fanciful notion that Baxendale had a shred of power to make her aware of nothing but him.

'I'll see you to your car,' Greville was just saying as they went to go through the double door, when some man Greville knew stopped him and seemed to want 'just a moment' of his time on a small matter of business.

A businesswoman herself, albeit just now an ex-businesswoman, Astra knew full well that a 'moment' could mean an age. She was quite capable of seeing herself to her car.

'Be in touch,' she said lightly, kissed her cousin's cheek, and went out into the hall.

She didn't make it to the outer door before she was pounced on by the man who had introduced himself as Leigh Jenkins. He was still only *thinking* of going home, then?

'I didn't get your name?' He plonked himself straight in front of her, and looked as if he had no intention of moving until she supplied her name.

'No, you didn't,' she answered, and went to go by round him.

He caught hold of her arm to stop her—she objected most strongly to being manhandled. She froze him with a look, and he had the grace to let go of her arm. 'What's a guy have to do to get a date with you?' he asked peevishly.

Had he been other than the brash, pushy type, Astra might well have softened her refusal. But he *was* pushy, he was brash—and she hadn't missed him ogling her several times that evening. Were it not for the fact that she and Greville had stayed comfortably close together, she had an idea he would have tried his luck earlier. So, 'You don't!' she told him icily, and brushed past him to the outer door.

She didn't immediately get to go through that door, however, because some other man had come out into the hall, and, by the look of things, had overheard every word of her conversation with Leigh Jenkins.

'Now there's a girl who lives up to her nickname,' drawled a voice she was not a stranger to. And while she hesitated, her hand already down by the door handle, Sayre Baxendale strolled over to her, placing himself in between her and Leigh Jenkins.

She went to reach for the door handle, but, as Leigh Jenkins melted away, so, against all her instincts, she stayed where she was to face Sayre Baxendale. She'd be damned if she'd let him think that because of his low opinion of her she was running away.

'I haven't a nickname,' she denied coldly. If he'd invented one for her—she didn't want to know it.

'That's not what I heard,' he mocked, his dark gaze flicking over her, taking in her cool, elegant deportment, her fine features and upswept red hair.

Astra was momentarily shaken. The only nickname she'd got—and since she'd left Yarroll Finance that would have left with her—was the one she'd been dubbed with while working there. But surely he couldn't know... Yet—hadn't she just been more than a touch frosty with Leigh Jenkins? Was that what Baxendale was referring to—North Pole Northcott?

'Norman Davis wrote to you?' She took a stab in the dark—surely to goodness her ex-boss wouldn't have mentioned that nickname in any letter, even if he knew it, which she doubted. He was much more professional than that.

'I don't recall hearing from any Norman Davis,' Sayre Baxendale replied. 'Though I do believe I received a communication from a Maurice Robertson.'

Good grief! They didn't come any higher up in Yarroll Finance than Maurice Robertson! In an instant Astra saw how it had been. Norman Davis had reported her oversight to his superior, mentioned the name Sayre Baxendale, as he naturally would, and so it had gone higher yet higher, until Maurice Robertson had heard of it.

'I hardly think Mr Robertson would be so unprofessional as to bandy nicknames in any business letter thanking you for your interest,' Astra tilted her chin to tell him haughtily.

Sayre Baxendale's eyes narrowed for a brief moment, letting her know—as if she cared—that he wasn't too enamoured by her uppity manner. Then that mocking look was back. 'Neither did he,' he drawled. 'Apparently you were recommended to Ronald Cummings via Veronica

Edwards, through a friend of hers who works for Yarroll Finance. The same friend passed on the good news to Veronica that North Pole Northcott no longer worked for the company. Tell me,' he went on, retribution his in full for her daring to have come the high and mighty with him, 'what are you doing now you've been dismissed for incompetence?'

Had he deliberately been trying to goad her, he did a splendid job. 'You've been misinformed!' Astra snapped, angry pink colour flushing her normally pale cheeks. 'When I found some of the people I was called upon to deal with too obnoxious for words I *resigned.*' Chew on that!

She had as good as called him obnoxious—it glanced off him. 'You're still in the same line of business?' he enquired silkily. 'You *are* working, I take it?'

Odious—obnoxious was too good for him! 'I've had two good offers,' she took great delight in being able to inform him. He wasn't to know that both offers were in the family, so to speak, or that both offers of a job were for the one firm.

'You've accepted neither?' Dark, all-assessing eyes studied her. Why did she feel she'd love to poke him in the eye? She'd never had such tendencies before!

'I'm being selective,' she replied coolly, in control of her anger once more. Her control didn't stay around for long.

How could it? He strained it to the limits when loftily he suggested, 'You obviously earned enough commission in your last job not to need to take another job for a while.'

What *was* it about this man? Astra took a long, steadying breath. She'd be hanged if she'd tell him she had private means. 'Obviously,' she agreed, her temper straining at the leash. She opened the door—to the devil with him; she was going home.

Before she could so much as take a step outside, however, Baxendale was there again with his comments.

Though she had to admit she was a touch baffled by his change of subject when he said, 'You and Alford seem on very close terms?'

What on earth had her cousin Greville Alford got to do with any of this? Astra threw Baxendale a look of intense dislike. 'We are,' she replied coldly. 'Very close.' And, not giving him a chance to get another remark in, she went swiftly through the door and marched over the tarmac drive.

Honestly! That man! Never had any man upset her the way he so easily did. Insufferable swine! The next time Greville invited her to a party, she'd ask to see the guest list first. If Sayre Baxendale's name were on it, Greville would be going on his own!

CHAPTER THREE

GREVILLE telephoned Astra on Sunday morning to enquire
if she got home all right. 'I would have rung you last night,
only I got held up longer than I expected. Did you enjoy
the party?'

Greville himself gave fabulous parties. By comparison
the one they'd attended last night was average. 'More to
the point, did you?'

'Yes,' he said simply, and Astra didn't miss that there
was a smile in his voice.

'When are you seeing her again?'

'Ah—slight snag.'

'You didn't ask her out?' Astra was surprised—her
cousin was normally self-assured, confident—he really had
got it badly.

'I didn't get very much of a chance last night,' Greville
owned. 'Her brother was there and, albeit he wasn't always
at her side, I thought he seemed a mite protective of her.'

'How old is she?' Astra enquired, wondering if the
woman her cousin was so enamoured with might be some
giddy young woman.

'Late twenties, maybe thirty,' Greville replied, and
should Astra think that thirty was a bit mature to have a
brother watching over her he was instantly defensive of his
love. 'She's been through a very tough time lately,' he explained.

'I'm sorry.'

'Don't be—you're gorgeous,' he answered, and was back
to being her super cousin again, who, if truth be told, had

done a fair job of watching over his three cousins in their traumatic growing years.

The week began slowly and dully, but Astra was cheered on Thursday to receive a postcard from Fennia. 'Yancie was right,' she read. 'S'wonderful.' They had received a 'S'wonderful' card from Yancie on her honeymoon.

Astra was still smiling when her phone suddenly called for attention. It was her cousin Greville again. 'Anything wrong?' she asked. Although they were regularly in touch and knew each other's happenings, either via his mother, her mother, her other cousins or her aunts, sometimes an age could go by without Greville phoning.

'Why should anything be wrong? Can't I ring my lovely cousin to enquire how she's feeling without there being something wrong?'

'So your lovely cousin's fine. She's not fretting because she's not working a sixteen-hour day. And no, she hasn't yet found another job that has the same appeal as the last one, but she hasn't seriously been looking.' Astra took a breath, and then asked gently, 'So, what's troubling you, love?'

There was a second or two of silence before Greville, the pretence over, the game up, told her the real reason for his call. 'I need a favour.'

He was the dearest man. 'It's yours,' she answered unequivocally. Should that favour be another party with even the remotest possibility of Sayre Baxendale attending—she could be equivocal later. That fiend Baxendale had been in and out of her head ever since Saturday's party—before that even—and she'd had enough of him. But, for the moment, Greville was sounding a touch anxious, and it would be a pleasure to help him for a change. 'What can I do for you?' she offered cheerfully.

'Would you come to the theatre with me tomorrow?'

Astra had always known how much Greville enjoyed the

theatre and was ready to say straight away that she'd be pleased to go with him. But she sensed there was more to his wish that she accompany him tomorrow than hoping she would enjoy it.

'I don't know her name, but she'll be there, won't she? The woman you...'

'Ellen,' he supplied. Astra did a quick flip through a name-and-picture gallery of the women he had introduced her to on Saturday, but she couldn't link 'Ellen' to any of them. 'Ellen Morton,' Greville went on, her name sounding gentle on his tongue. 'The thing is, Astra, I rang Ellen on Tuesday asking her to have dinner with me—and got a polite refusal for my trouble.'

'Oh, Greville. Don't give up hope,' Astra encouraged.

'I won't. This is much too serious for that. The problem is, though, and you'll call me all sorts of a clod, I bumped into Nick Wilson today—he was at the party on Saturday—and he remarked on my stunning partner. But when I said you weren't my partner but my cousin he said that if he'd known he wouldn't have been poaching he'd have come over and asked if you'd any space in your diary to fit him in. He asked for your phone number, by the way.'

'You didn't give it to him!'

'Would I? Though he deserves some reward, because if it wasn't for him I wouldn't have got round to wondering had I mentioned to Ellen when I introduced you that you were my cousin. Had I, in fact, told anybody at that party that we were cousins?'

Astra tried to remember—but all she could remember was that she had told Sayre Baxendale that she and Greville were very close, but definitely hadn't told Baxendale that they were cousins. 'I don't think you did,' she confessed slowly after a few seconds.

She heard Greville groan. Then suddenly he brightened. Though he did start off by confessing, 'I'm in such a stew,

I don't seem to be able to think straight any more. But follow me through this, Astra. If some chap came up to you at a party and introduced a beautiful redhead, and then—given that the chap exchanged a few pleasantries with you every now and then—more or less stayed glued near to said redhead all night... Then—bearing in mind you'd had your fill of philandering Casanovas, having a year ago divorced one—how would you react if a few days later the redhead's seeming-to-be boyfriend rang you up and asked you to dine with him?'

Astra knew that she'd tell any such man to go take a running jump. But Greville was suffering here. 'Do I like this man?' she asked.

'I wish I knew,' Greville groaned. 'I don't feel I can ring her again just to say, Oh, by the way, the beautiful redhead's my cousin. I'd feel a complete idiot. Besides which, with her ex-husband being such a Don Juan, the poor girl's probably heard a dozen or more similar lines in her day, and wouldn't believe me, anyway.'

Astra saw the light. 'But if I went with you to the theatre tomorrow night...'

'I'd angle to be somewhere near Ellen during the interval—with you right there beside me, of course. Then I could say, casually You know my cousin, Astra, don't you? and...'

'Hey presto, you'll hope your next phone call will be more favourably received. What time do you want me to be ready?'

'You're a darling. But I always knew that—despite that detached air you show everybody else.'

Astra put the phone down after Greville's call, hardly crediting the change that had come over her cousin. All through her life she had known him as kind and caring, and had also known him as sophisticated but sociable—though careful since the end of his marriage to never again

let anyone get too close. But look at him now! He'd known
in advance that Ellen Morton would be at the party, but as
soon as he'd been in the same room with her—his normally
clever brain had scrambled! He hadn't even remembered to
introduce his cousin as his cousin!

If falling in love did that to you, and to Astra it sounded
as if Greville was up to his ears in love, then she was glad
she'd decided to have nothing whatsoever to do with that
emotion.

Though she did so want Greville to be happy. He had
been through such a terrible time. By the look of it Ellen
Morton had been on the same ghastly treadmill of broken
marriage too. Wouldn't it be wonderful if Ellen Morton
could learn to love Greville? Astra knew that her cousin
had had many lady-friends since his divorce, but inside his
marriage he had been faithful; none had been more trust-
worthy.

There was a school of thought that said everything went
in threes. Yancie had married, Fennia had married—perhaps Greville... Grief! Astra brought herself up short; she
was getting to be a romantic! Her cousin hadn't even managed to get a date with the woman yet, and here she was
marrying them off!

Even though Greville was early calling for her the following evening, Astra—wearing a straight dress of green
silk—was ready. She sensed he was nervous, anxious and
on edge, so purposely chatted calmly to him all the way to
the theatre.

The strain was starting to show even as they took their
seats. 'I do hope she'll come,' he said worriedly. And a
few minutes later he remarked, 'She sounded all right when
I spoke to her on the phone, but there's a lot of summer
colds about.'

'She'll be here,' Astra answered lightly, wondering how

the dickens he was going to last until the interval when the performance hadn't even started yet!

Greville 'accidentally' dropped his programme, and in bending to pick it up took an 'uninterested' scan around. 'She's here!' he mumbled in Astra's ear as he bent to take his seat, and sounded so tense that for an awful moment she had a dreadful idea that his love was here with some other man.

'Ellen's here with her brother?' Astra asked lightly, calmly, recalling how last Sunday Greville had said Ellen had been at the party with her protective brother.

'She's with Sayre and the Listers,' Greville answered, keeping his voice low.

Sayre! Astra felt her scalp tingle. It couldn't be! 'Sayre?' she enquired, her light, calm tone threatening to escape.

'Sayre Baxendale, Ellen's brother,' Greville supplied. 'Didn't I introduce you?'

Astra was normally calm without effort. 'I don't believe you did,' she replied—and her cousin would never know the effort it cost her to keep her voice even.

'That's splendid!' he exclaimed, only just holding a lid on his emotions. 'I'll introduce him to my cousin in the interval—he'll be delighted to meet you.' Astra doubted it.

The house lights went down, and she wanted to go home. Oh, what rotten, rotten luck! Her dear cousin had gone and fallen for that odious man's sister! And she, Astra Northcott, commission hunter to the point of criminality, according to the odious Baxendale, was expected to smile nicely and say 'how d'you do' to him. Oh, botheration!

It was only by reminding herself that she was there that evening because her cousin wanted, in pursuance of his love, to repair omissions that she stayed in her seat. What the play was about passed her by. For Greville's sake, she was going to have to stick it out. It was to be hoped,

though, that Baxendale had sufficient manners in company
to keep any insulting comments to himself.

Sophisticated or no, Greville was one of the first out of
his seat when the interval came. 'It's a good play,' remarked she who had little idea what it was about as she
stood in the bar nursing a gin and tonic while Greville held
a Scotch and 'casually' observed fellow members of the
audience piling in.

'Very good,' he replied, and Astra guessed he had taken
in about as much of what the play had been about as she
had. 'Ah, Ellen!' he exclaimed, as a fair-haired, blue-eyed
woman came near. 'May I get you something to drink?'

'Sayre's got it all arranged, I think,' she smiled, and was
about to move on. Greville wasn't having that.

'You know Astra, don't you?' he smiled, and Astra had
to admire that nobody would know how churned up inside
he was about this woman.

But he wasn't the only one who was churned up inside.
Sayre Baxendale and the people he was with came over to
his sister's side. His dark glance raked over Astra, standing
straight-backed and cool, while Ellen pleasantly answered,
'We met at the Westlakes' party.'

Astra smiled and was about to make some conventional
statement on how very nice the party had been when
Greville, having greeted Sayre and the couple he was with,
smiled at Astra and said, 'Astra, I don't recall introducing
Sayre Baxendale on Saturday.' And, shifting his smile to
the other man, he continued, 'Sayre, I don't think you know
my cousin, Astra Northcott.'

Dark eyes bored into hers—Astra stared back, unblinking, but didn't make the mistake this time of extending a
hand to him. Though, for Greville's sake, she inclined her
head a cool fraction. 'Hello,' she managed, and looked past
him as Greville introduced her to the other couple, Kit and
Vanessa Lister.

Astra was generally quite comfortable conversing with people, and as they each sipped their drinks she chatted easily to the two women, who happened to be nearest. She liked them both, and took to Ellen Morton and her gentle manner. But the whole while Astra couldn't help but be conscious of Sayre Baxendale.

She supposed she must give him credit for having a few manners, in that when she would have thought him easily capable of moving his party away he remained sociably with them. Nor had he told her cousin that they had already met, or indeed added anything in his own inimitable unpleasant style.

But the interval, in Astra's opinion, seemed to be going on for ever. She had never been particularly conscious of any male, but—perhaps because of her previous two unpleasant experiences with Sayre Baxendale—she was aware of him the whole of the time.

She was never more glad when the bell rang to indicate the play would resume again very shortly. 'We'd better get back,' Kit Lister said to his wife, and he and Vanessa moved into the dawdling mass making their way back to their seats.

Astra had to hide a smile when she saw how, so inconspicuously she hadn't noticed, her cousin had manoeuvred himself next to Ellen Morton, so that, as the throng thickened and the Listers became separated from their small group, Greville had Ellen to himself.

Astra saw him exchange comments with Ellen and, wanting to give him every opportunity for private conversation, she hung back.

There was not a smile about Astra a few seconds later, however, when she discovered that, in her desire to give Greville an opportunity of a few minutes with Ellen, she had completely overlooked the possibility that she might have Sayre Baxendale breathing down her neck.

She decided, best manners no longer required, to ignore him. Then found he was not so easy to ignore when a voice she could well do without hearing drawled, 'So why didn't you tell me that Alford was your cousin?'

She shrugged, aware that Baxendale was referring to her agreement at the party that she and Greville were very close. 'Why should I tell you anything?' she challenged. 'I thought you knew it all!' she added acidly.

It pleased her to get that little dig in. Her pleasure was short-lived. The people in front halted, causing everyone else to wait while the congestion sorted itself out. Astra sensed as she too stopped that the black-haired man was looking down at her—he could look all he liked; she wasn't looking up.

That was, to look up had never been her intention. But that was before, ignoring her acid, Sayre Baxendale bent and murmured in her ear, 'Talking of knowing all there is to know—I'm reliably informed that you're frigid.'

Shaken rigid, her head jerked up. Mocking dark eyes stared into wide green eyes. He, she saw, as his glance went to her mouth, seemed to be pleasantly satisfied at the way her mouth had fallen open in shock.

Hastily she pulled herself together. 'I don't believe you've been reliably informed of any such thing,' she accused loftily.

'You deny it?' he questioned, clearly not bothered a jot that she had just more or less called him a liar. And when she tilted her head a haughty fraction he continued, 'You'd have me believe that the name of North Pole Northcott is entirely unearned?'

The throng began to move again. 'Believe what the devil you like!' Astra snapped. 'I promise you, you'd be the very last to find out.'

'Very kind—but if you don't mind I'd sooner sleep in the deep freeze.'

That man! Astra acknowledged she knew little of what the first half of the play had been about; when, inwardly fuming, she reached her seat, she was to know nothing of what the rest of the play was about.

Oh, what a swine the man was! Only then, away from the ghastly monster, could she see that, while he might be aware of her 'North Pole Northcott' nickname, he hadn't at all been 'reliably' informed that she was frigid. What he hadn't cared for was her acid remark 'I thought you knew it all!' That being so, he had deliberately decided to shock her.

And not only that, but when she'd attempted to cut him down to size by telling him that he'd be the very last to find out he'd as good as said he'd sooner sleep in the deep freeze than sleep with her.

In the month that followed, Astra's calls from Greville were much more frequent than in the past. It could have been that, because he knew she was no longer working, he felt more free to engage her in long conversations over the phone. But since they always seemed to end up talking about Ellen, Astra realised that, since she knew of his feelings for Ellen Morton, when he felt the need to talk to someone in confidence about his lack of progress with Ellen, his cousin cared enough to be a willing ear.

'It looks as though it might be Christmas before I manage to get a date with her,' he'd said only last night. 'If then!'

Christmas was a good three months away. But, from what her cousin said, he did manage to be in Ellen's company at least once a week when they—at Greville's express design—bumped into each other at some function or other. So, albeit always with other people there, he did manage to spend some time chatting to her.

'Don't be down-hearted,' Astra advised. 'You understand better than most how devastating it is when your marriage ends.'

'I know, I know. But it has been a year now since her divorce—' He broke off, as if realising the many years it had taken him to get over his broken marriage. 'It's just that I want to look after her, take care of her...'

'Didn't you say that her brother was doing a very good job there?'

'Sayre,' he replied. Astra preferred not to speak the unspeakable man's name. 'The man's remarkable! Somehow, while not depriving himself of glamorous female company, he still manages to watch out for Ellen.'

Very commendable, Astra felt sure, and wished in the couple of hours that followed that she had not mentioned Ellen's brother—she couldn't get the detestable man out of her mind. She wasn't frigid—was she?

Well, what if she was? Frigid surely was much better than being like her free-with-her-favours mother—not to mention her aunts. Not Aunt Delia, of course. Apart from her cousins, Aunt Delia was her only true and steady relative.

Not forgetting her father, though, a man of utmost integrity. On impulse she went to the phone and rang him. He was pleased to hear from her and, after chatting for some minutes, he again asked her out to Barbados and they discussed a notion she'd been toying with of training for an entirely different career.

'You want to stay out of finance?'

'I fouled up with Yarroll's—I wouldn't want to work with any firm who didn't match up to their high standards. Which would probably mean, since I'd have to tell any prospective new employer why I left my last job, that any firm of high standing wouldn't care to employ me.'

Her father commiserated for a moment before asking, 'You're still set on a career?'

'I think so. I thoroughly enjoyed being a part of Yarroll Finance.'

'There's no man in the offing, then?' he teased.

'Honestly!' she scolded, and—more peculiar than peculiar—thought of a pair of dark eyes on a black-haired, good-looking man who accused her—for all he made out it wasn't his accusation but someone else's—of being frigid. Swiftly and with all speed she ejected all thought of Sayre Baxendale from her mind. As if she'd want him for a man friend! Grief! 'Give me a career any time,' she laughed.

'Don't forget to play as well as work,' her father instructed.

Astra prowled restlessly around her immaculately clean and tidy apartment after her phone call. She felt restless, unsettled. Perhaps the fact that she had done nothing about a new career yet was because she hadn't fully come to terms with the way her old job had ended.

Perhaps she would go and pay her father a visit. Perhaps after a holiday she would return in a more settled frame of mind, and be ready and eager to take on new challenges.

Astra felt much brighter on Wednesday when, with Fennia now back from her honeymoon, she and Yancie came to the apartment for lunch.

'Don't tell me how you are,' Astra addressed Fennia after hugging both her cousins. 'You look radiant.'

'Doesn't she, though?' Yancie chimed in.

'You don't look so bad in the radiance stakes yourself, Yancie,' Fennia grinned.

'You're both disgustingly blissful,' Astra complained, was hugged by both of them for her trouble, and had to laugh.

It was one of the happiest days she could remember since she and her job had parted company. And she was sorry to see her cousins go. But they were husband-oriented, and much though they'd laughed and talked, and laughed and talked some more, her two married cousins were happy to go home.

Astra was on the point of ringing her father a couple of days later to say she was about to book her flight, when her mother unexpectedly called to see her. Astra didn't like to be suspicious, but while wanting, quite desperately sometimes, to think only good of her parent events sadly proved otherwise. The last time her mother had dropped in on her it was because she had fancied a holiday in Barbados and, since her ex-husband had an extremely palatial home out there, didn't see why she should spend her funds on a hotel. She had contacted Carleton Northcott, but he had politely informed her he'd rather go swimming with sharks than have her to stay. She had subsequently called on her daughter and more or less ordered her to phone her father and ask him—at his daughter's special request—to change his mind.

Fortunately, Astra hadn't had to worry about what she should do for very long because, while her mother had still been there, her father had called from Barbados to say that her mother had phoned and it had suddenly occurred to him that his ex—and thank goodness for that—might well put pressure on Astra to do her dirty work.

'Er—Mother's here now, actually,' Astra had to confess—that or try to field her father's comments about the woman he had never loved, and had grown to actively dislike, as best she could.

'Is she, now?' he exclaimed sharply, knowing Imogen Kirby quite well enough to know what she was up to. 'Perhaps you'd like to let me speak to her?' he suggested nicely.

Astra, for all she wasn't fooled by his benign tone, passed the phone over to her mother. When her mother's initially sweet tone to her ex-husband started to sour as

Carleton Northcott didn't hold back from accusing her of still being as manipulative as ever—and from sour her mother went to shrieking at him—so Astra went to the kitchen to make some coffee.

The sound of the outer door slamming, and the ensuing silence, had told Astra that not only had the call from Barbados been terminated, but that her mother would not be stopping for coffee.

'How are you?' Astra asked now, inviting her mother in.

'You're still wearing your hair up in that same old hairstyle, I see,' Imogen Kirby complained in answer. And before Astra had done more than lead the way to the drawing room and invited her mother to take a seat she began, 'Delia told me today that you've given up your job.'

'That's right,' Astra replied evenly, gratefully aware that her aunt Delia would have imparted none of the regret Astra had felt about that, nor that she hadn't had any option but to give up her job.

'So you'll be going out to stay with your father for a while?'

Subtle her mother could be, but not where her daughter was concerned, Astra realised. 'Where did you get that idea?' she hedged, knowing what was coming.

'I rang him.'

'You rang him?' After last time? Her mother, it seemed, was determined to have her free month or two in Barbados.

'I rang him after I'd seen Delia today. It's all very well him being thousands of miles away—I thought he should do something about looking after you.'

Astra stared at her elegant mother in amazement. Of the two, her father had always taken much greater care of her. 'Mother, I'm twenty-two!' she gasped. Grief, she'd been out in the big wide career world for two years. What was her mother thinking of, ringing her father like that? Astra very soon found out.

Imogen Kirby ignored her daughter's amazement, and went directly to the purpose of her call. 'Carleton Northcott told me,' said she who had once been married to him, 'that he'd asked you to go to him for a holiday. I think you should go.'

And take you with me! Apart from her father's horror at the very idea, a week with her selfish mother, let alone a month, and Astra knew she'd be ready to join him in shark-infested waters. 'Didn't Aunt Delia tell me you've just been on holiday?' Astra queried—actually it had been Greville who'd told her, but it amounted to the same thing. Apparently, her mother had not gone alone. Astra doubted that her companion had been a female of the species.

Imogen Kirby, who hadn't yet mentioned accompanying her daughter to Barbados, sent her a look of dislike. 'That's no reason why I can't have another holiday!' she retorted.

Astra's decision was made. It might make her mother happy to have a free trip to Barbados—but it would make her father extremely upset. 'I've decided to stay in London and find myself another job,' she stated.

'That's the most ludicrous thing I ever heard,' her mother snapped, thoroughly disgruntled. Astra withstood a ten-minute bombardment on what she should and should not do, how she did not need the money—with a couple of 'ungratefuls' thrown in. But, when her mother could see she was getting nowhere, she angrily departed.

Astra, still feeling guilty as she usually did after one of her mother's visits, spent Sunday with her aunt Delia. It was a glorious summer's day and they were having tea on the lawn when her aunt asked if she had seen anything of Greville recently.

'Not recently,' Astra answered truthfully.

'Did he seem—um—a little preoccupied when last you saw him?'

Dearly did Astra want to tell her aunt as much as she

knew—but wasn't sure how Greville would feel. 'Er—how do you mean?' she prevaricated.

And was on the receiving end of Delia Alford's thoughtful look, a moment before she asked, 'What do you know that I don't?'

'I...' Astra couldn't lie to her, and never loved her aunt more when, even though Greville was the brightest light in his mother's life, Delia Alford didn't press her too hard. 'I don't want you to break any confidences. Just tell me—is he happy?'

'I think so,' Astra answered. And, realising at once that that answer might leave her aunt worrying, she blurted out, 'He's interested in someone, and...' She stopped abruptly.

'He's interested...' Her aunt was suddenly smiling. Even as she apologised, 'I'm sorry, Astra, I rather pushed you into that,' she was smiling. The news Astra had given her was obviously good news. 'I won't ask anything else, I promise. Well,' she amended, 'perhaps... Have you met her?' Astra nodded. 'Is she nice?'

'Very,' Astra answered—shame about the brother. Stop thinking about him—it's ridiculous!

'Then I'll sit on my curiosity until my son feels he can tell me more himself. Now, how about some fresh tea?'

Astra tried to ring Greville when she got home. It seemed to be her week for feeling guilty. But he wasn't in. She thought better than to ring him at his office the next day, but managed to contact him early that evening.

'I was just about to ring you,' he said before she could get her confession in.

'I tried to contact you last night.'

'I was out—at a dinner party,' Greville answered, and sounded so pleased with life just then that Astra was pretty certain that Ellen Morton had been amongst the guests.

'I was with your mother yesterday,' Astra began, wanting to get her confession said and over.

Only it seemed that what Greville had been going to ring her about wouldn't wait. 'How do you fancy spending the weekend in the country?'

Astra quite liked the idea. 'Tell me more,' she said—and was promptly dumbfounded at his astonishing reply.

'Ellen—well, Sayre actually—and I can hardly believe my luck—has invited us to spend this coming weekend at Abberley; that's the name of his house. Ellen's living at Abberley—did I mention that?' He went on when Astra, too shaken to speak, made no answer. 'You remember Sayre Baxendale,' Greville prodded. Remember him! She was never likely to forget him! 'You remember, that night at the theatre. That night I...'

'Yes, I remember.' She managed to find her voice. But, *'Us!'* she exclaimed, getting her breath back. 'You don't mean...'

'I mean us—you and me,' Greville confirmed. And still she didn't believe it.

'You're saying Sayre Baxendale has invited *me,* as well as you?' She sought more definite confirmation.

'That's what I'm saying. It'll be great, won't it?' Greville raced on enthusiastically. 'Almost two whole days in Ellen's company—our friendship's bound to progress. I'm sure she likes me. I could hardly believe it when Sayre asked me. We'll go down Friday evening. I'll call for you at...'

'Greville. I can't go!' Astra interrupted his eagerness before he should get it any more firmly established in his mind.

'You can't go?' Greville questioned, sounding extremely surprised. 'I sort of got the idea that you weren't doing anything very special this weekend? You'll love it, Astra; honestly you will. There'll be quite a party of us, with some sort of horsey thing going on not too far away on Saturday. You like horses, I know you...'

'But I hardly *know* them. Him.' Astra rapidly backed away. No *way* was she going to go anywhere near Sayre Baxendale's home that weekend.

'But...'

'I'm sorry, Greville,' Astra cut in, starting to feel she might be letting her cousin down, while something stronger inside assured her that since Greville had been in the company of Ellen and her brother very recently—and Astra had seen neither in over a month—it was obviously Greville, and only Greville, that they really wanted at Abberley that weekend. 'I'm sure he—S-Sayre—has only invited me out of courtesy.'

'Oh, Astra. Come on! He mentioned you by name. He'd really like you to join in the fun.'

Like a hole in the head he would. She wished she could lie to her cousin and invent something else she was doing that weekend. 'I'm sorry,' she repeated, feeling more and more certain that since she knew for a fact the very low opinion Baxendale had of her it must surely be his sister who had asked him to invite her. For himself, he'd rather emigrate than have her over his threshold. 'I just don't feel comfortable about accepting an invitation that wasn't extended to me *personally*. Anyhow, my not going won't stop you going, will it?'

'For the chance to spend two days with Ellen, wild horses wouldn't stop me,' he answered honestly.

'Have a lovely time,' she bade him, and, wanting to rapidly change the subject, had one handy which she could no longer avoid. 'I was with Aunt Delia yesterday, as I mentioned,' Astra began. 'I owe you another apology,' she admitted.

'What have you done?'

Astra came away from the phone feeling much relieved that Greville had taken lightly her confession that she'd let out to his parent he was interested in someone. Probably with this coming weekend and the prospect of spending so much time with Ellen Morton to the forefront of his mind Greville felt anything else was inconsequential.

Relieved though she was that Greville wasn't angry with her, Astra was nevertheless plagued by her conscience. Greville had never, ever let *her* down. But, by refusing to go to Baxendale's home with him, she had let her cousin down.

Would it have hurt her so much to have gone? She wasn't scared of the wretched man, for goodness' sake! But—why should she go? She had already established that nothing, hell nor high water, would prevent Greville from going. So he didn't really need to take her along with him.

Just the same, Astra was still feeling a touch guilty a couple of days later. She took up the evening paper, deciding that what she needed to do was occupy her mind. Perhaps there'd be a job position in the employment ads that might appeal.

She had barely opened the paper, however, when Security phoned to say that there was a gentleman there asking to see her. 'Is it all right for me to let him come up?'

Astra wasn't expecting anybody, and the men on Security all knew Greville. 'Does he have a name?' she enquired.

There was a pause while her question was put to her visitor. Then Astra was nearly dropping with shock when the information came. 'It's a Mr Baxendale.'

Her mouth fell open, her thoughts went chaotic. To her mind there was only one Baxendale; she had no need to enquire of his first name. Instinctively she wanted to say she wasn't in—but Baxendale knew that she was. No way was she going to give him the satisfaction of knowing that she was nervous of... Nervous? Oh, for heaven's sake.

'Send him up,' she requested without thinking further.

Astra put down the phone, looked at what she was wearing and was halfway to her bedroom to change when she came to an abrupt halt. For goodness' sake—what was wrong with her? She was dressed perfectly fine for an evening at home. There was nothing whatsoever the matter with her tailored trousers and silk shirt. She hadn't invited him; let him take her as he found her.

But, having instructed herself thus, Astra just the same went to a mirror and checked that her hair was neatly, not to say as elegantly as ever, swept up immaculately in the chignon her mother so disliked.

The doorbell sounded. Astra went to answer it. But, and most oddly, she found she had to take a deep and controlling breath before, her cool and aloof image safely to the fore, she opened the door to her unexpected visitor.

He was as she remembered him. Tall, dark and, she reluctantly again admitted, good-looking. He held out his hand. Oh, wasn't life grand? With utmost pleasure, she ignored it. 'Come in,' she said—and made the mistake of looking into his eyes. She had supposed they would be frosty—she guessed it wasn't every day that someone refused to shake hands with him. But, instead of looking annoyed by her action, as she'd hoped, if her eyes weren't deceiving her, he looked more amused than anything else.

Astra tilted her chin a haughty fraction, and led the way into the drawing room. She had no idea why Baxendale had called to see her, but no doubt he would soon tell her. She debated whether to invite him to sit down.

'Nice place you have here,' he remarked before she had come to a decision, his glance taking in the elegance of the room, the fine pictures on the walls, the lush carpeting and fittings. The room, in fact, tastefully suggested that money was no object.

'It's amazing what one can do with a bit of commission,' she murmured pleasantly—and again expected frost.

It seemed to be her evening for disappointments. There
was not an atom of frost about Sayre Baxendale. He was
even quite pleasant himself as he acknowledged her unhid-
den dig.

'I deserved that,' he accepted.

That rather took the wind out of her sails. She rallied.
'I'd offer you a drink, only I'm sure you're in a hurry to
be elsewhere,' she hinted.

'Coffee, black, no sugar,' he answered, to her astonishment. To her further astonishment she found she had moved
a couple of paces in the direction of the kitchen to make
it!

Knowing she would feel a complete fool if she halted,
Astra carried on walking. What *was* it about this man?
Well, she still wasn't going to ask him to sit down. He
could drink it standing up!

'You've no need at all to work, have you?'

Come into the kitchen, why don't you? She'd no idea
that he had followed her. Though she refused to let her
indignation show, and busied herself with the coffee the
sooner to get rid of him. Why was he here anyway? A
ghastly thought suddenly struck her—if things went well
with Greville and Ellen, this odious man could end up being some kind of in-law to her! Oh, Greville, don't do that
to me, *please*.

'Since you mention it, no,' she replied evenly, and found
she had poured two cups of coffee and placed them on a
tray, 'though the apartment isn't mine; it belongs to my
father.'

Sayre Baxendale took the tray from her and stood back
so she should precede him. 'You live here with your father?' he enquired conversationally, when in the drawing
room, he placed the tray down on a low table, and handed
her a cup she had never wanted in the first place—she had
absolutely no idea why she had made coffee for two. She'd

had just about enough of him. So why did she sit down—giving him a chance to follow suit?

'My father lives in Barbados.' Civility cost nothing.

'He lives there with your mother?'

Honestly! 'My parents are divorced,' Astra answered, her civility starting to slip. She sent Baxendale a sharp look—he received it with a smile.

'Word has reached me that you don't go anywhere without a personal invitation,' he remarked, and the crux of why he was there, why he had come to see her, suddenly arrived.

'You've never come here tonight just to personally invite me to your home this weekend?' she exclaimed, knowing full well that he couldn't give a fig whether she went to his home, Abberley, on Friday or where she went.

'Why else would you suppose I've come?' he questioned, his dark eyes going from her wide green eyes to take in her flawless complexion and shining red hair.

'You can't possibly want me in your home,' she declared.

'What I want, what I'm trying to do, is to get Ellen back to the person she was before her marriage broke up and she retired into some kind of shell, where she changed from a happy, sociable woman into a timid mouse and seems content to stay there.'

'Perhaps she's happy there—in her shell.'

'I know her—she isn't,' he replied shortly.

'Why are you telling me this?' Astra questioned.

He looked at her levelly, not a glimmer of amusement about him, then, to her surprise, he answered, 'I know, through my dealings with you, that anything I tell you will be treated as confidential.' Her eyes widened yet further. 'Ellen has been through a great deal of emotional trauma which so took its toll, she had a breakdown.'

'Oh, I'm so sorry!' Astra exclaimed softly.

'While from somewhere she found the strength to cut her

worthless husband out from her life and ultimately divorce him, the experience and all that led up to it so shattered her that she wanted to hide away from the world. Ellen's now starting to recover. I want it to continue.'

'Which is what this weekend at your place is all about?'

'If I didn't think she'd enjoy it, I wouldn't have suggested it. But she's been out and about quite a bit now. I think she's ready for a weekend with a few friends and...'

'I'm not a friend. I'm more of an acquaintance,' Astra put in.

'What you are is the cousin of a man with whom—and I've seen it for myself—Ellen feels comfortable with. I'd go as far as to say she appears more comfortable, more light-hearted, in Greville Alford's company than any other man's.'

'Greville's been through similar emotional trauma,' Astra felt she could reveal without betraying her cousin.

'So I believe,' Sayre Baxendale replied—and Astra had a feeling then that her cousin had been very thoroughly checked out by Baxendale. In the circumstances, she couldn't say she blamed him. 'It's immaterial at this stage whether Ellen and Greville Alford remain the comfortable friends they seem to be or move on from there. It's just my personal opinion that Ellen will feel even more relaxed, unthreatened if you like, by any hint of any closer friendship with him if you're at Abberley with him.'

Astra stared at Sayre Baxendale. 'Have I got this right?' she questioned.

'You're a clever woman—go on.'

'You are here to personally invite me to your home, in order that your sister will not get—um—perhaps a little panicky that Greville is paying her particular attention. Attention which, seeing the gentleman he is, Greville would divide between the two of us since he would never leave me to fend for myself.'

Baxendale burst out laughing. It was a pleasing sound. 'Forgive me,' he apologised at once, straightening his face. 'The idea of you—snooty, never a hair out of place, haughty beyond the point of arrogance—wilting at having to fend for yourself is a picture I can't quite conjure up.'

'Thank you very much!' she retorted sniffily.

'I've seen you in action squashing one male hopeful, remember,' he reminded her pleasantly.

Astra rather supposed he must be referring to that man at the party—Leigh something or other. But—arrogance! Baxendale could talk! 'So, for your sister's sake, you're prepared to have me under your roof this weekend? For...'

'Have you considered you too might actually enjoy it?' he butted in.

'The thought had never occurred to me!' she told him loftily—realising straight away that the arrogance he had spoken of was showing! So she changed tack completely to ask, 'You trust me? Despite accusing me of very near criminal activity in connection with your PA's father, you trust me?'

'I was wrong to so accuse you. I admit it,' he answered seriously.

She wanted to say 'Grovel'. What she did say—and thought herself most pathetic because of it—was, 'We both made a mistake, me by selling Mr Cummings the wrong plan, you by accusing me of doing it solely to gain a larger commission.'

'If it's any consolation to you, Astra,' Sayre Baxendale said charmingly, 'Veronica Edwards, my PA,' he reminded her in case she had forgotten the woman's name, 'is getting more and more embarrassed. Because I'd interfered I thought I should follow it through,' he owned. 'But my finance people are growing more and more fed up with this man they're trying to help, but who changes his mind every two days.' He smiled and Astra's heart did a little flip at how she preferred his devastating smile to his glower. 'I'm beginning to think that perhaps I should never have interfered to begin with,' he ended.

My, oh, my, was that an apology or was it? Astra's mouth started to pick up at the corners. Her lovely lips parted, revealing perfect white and even teeth; her full smile wouldn't be repressed. She smiled at Sayre Baxendale, and his glance went from her eyes down to her mouth, lingered, and then returned to her eyes.

Astra was still smiling as she asked, 'Where is Abberley, by the way?'

'Buckinghamshire,' he answered promptly. And, a steady look there in his dark eyes, he asked, 'You'll come?'

Astra hesitated—Sayre held her eyes, refusing to let her look away. 'Thank you, Sayre, I'd like to,' she heard herself say.

CHAPTER FOUR

AN HOUR after Sayre Baxendale's visit, Astra was starting to disbelieve that he had called at the apartment at all, much less that she had actually agreed to go to Abberley on Friday.

She rang her cousin. 'Thank you very much,' she said as soon as Greville answered the phone.

'It was a pleasure,' he answered teasingly, not a bit put out by her cool tone. 'What did I do?'

'Sayre Baxendale came to see me tonight—to ask me "personally" to go with you on Friday.'

'Did he, now?' Greville responded, sounding so genuinely surprised that Astra knew he'd had no idea that Sayre had intended to pay her a visit. 'And what did you answer, little sweeting?'

It was impossible for her to stay cross with Greville for very long. 'What time are you calling for me on Friday?' she laughed.

Friday came round exceedingly quickly and Astra could still hardly believe she had committed herself to spending a whole weekend in Sayre Baxendale's home. She didn't know if she even liked the man, so what was she doing packing a small case that would see her spending two nights under his roof?

How could she like him—he had called her snooty? That niggled away at her. No, she definitely didn't like him. He had a terrific smile, though— Oh, for goodness' sake, don't be so feeble.

While not having to try very hard to dislike him, Astra experienced a sudden rush of warm feeling towards him because he trusted her enough to confide what he had about his sister. She had an idea that he discussed Ellen with very few people.

Greville had left work early and called for her just after six. 'Apparently, because of everybody arriving in fits and starts, dinner will be a buffet affair.'

'Sounds a good idea,' Astra answered, and learned as they chatted and drove along that Greville had phoned Ellen on Monday to tell her that his cousin couldn't make it. However, unable to lie to Ellen, he'd found himself repeating what Astra had said about not feeling comfortable about accepting an invitation that wasn't extended to her personally.

'Ellen must have relayed that to Sayre,' Greville ended, and sounded so happy at the thought of staying in the same house as Ellen until Sunday morning that Astra could only wish everything good for him.

'You didn't give him my address?'

'I wouldn't need to. There are several sources he could use without contacting me.'

Abberley was a large old house, a sort of manor house, with thick stone walls, and set in its own grounds with masses of trees all around. That was Astra's first impression. She thought it lovely. Then the stout wooden door opened and Sayre Baxendale and his sister came out to greet them.

Sayre was casually dressed in shirt and trousers, and while Ellen, who was equally casually dressed, approached Astra and said how glad she was that Astra had come with Greville, Sayre shook hands with her cousin. Then Greville was greeting Ellen and taking a step or two away as the two exchanged a few pleasantries, and that was when Sayre came and stood in front of Astra.

For a second or two he just stared at her, trim and elegant in a trouser suit. He had shaken hands with her cousin but, remembering that the last time he had offered to shake hands with her she had ignored his offer, Astra wondered if he would try his luck a second time. She would, she knew, have shaken hands with him then—but she didn't get the chance.

Because, as they stared unsmiling at each other, suddenly Astra saw a kind of wicked look enter those dark eyes. The next she knew, making it look as if he greeted all female guests in this way, Sayre had caught a firm hold of her upper arms and, while she seemed too mesmerised to move, he bent and unhurriedly placed his lips against her cheek in a kiss of greeting.

Her cool, aloof, sophisticated image vanished in a moment. She pulled back, pushing him angrily away from her. *'Don't do that!'* she snapped, her cheek tingling.

'Well, if you're sure,' he replied affably, not a bit put out by her angry display. 'Welcome to Abberley,' he added pleasantly.

Had she been in her own car, Astra felt she might very well have told him to stuff Abberley and stormed out of there. But she wasn't in her car, she had come in Greville's, and, glancing over to where he stood, she could see he was so taken up with Ellen he had no idea his cousin was feeling sorely inclined to bash her host's head in. She was reminded that she wasn't here for her own benefit, even if Baxendale had suggested she might enjoy it.

It took a tremendous effort to overcome the intense, churned-up feelings going on inside her. But for Greville and his years of existing in an emotional wilderness, and for all the times he had 'been there' for her, Astra made that effort.

She swallowed hard, and stamped on the panicky feeling Baxendale's deliberate pay-back kiss had set off in her, and looked him straight in the eye. 'Your home is lovely, Sayre,' she smiled. 'I'm glad you persuaded me to come.'

And if you can't see that last sentence for the lie it is, you're not anywhere near as clever as I know you are.

He stared down at her, not by so much as a blink giving away that he knew she was lying through her teeth. 'Remind me to kiss you again some time,' he murmured.

'Remind me to duck,' she answered nicely.

It was Ellen who showed her to the room she would occupy in the vast house. 'I hope you'll be comfortable in here, but if there's anything you need do give me a shout.'

'It's a lovely room,' Astra answered truthfully—of the high-ceilinged, elegantly furnished room with its long windows overlooking extensive grounds. It had its own adjoining bathroom and, had she not still been feeling a trifle agitated by Sayre Baxendale's I'll-teach-you-not-to-not-shake-hands-with-me kiss, Astra felt she would absolutely love to be staying there.

She was taking a shower when she began to wonder what she had got so churned up inside about when Sayre had kissed her. Good heavens, it was only a kiss to her cheek. In a brave experiment in her teens, as if to discover if she had in fact inherited that promiscuous gene from the Jolliffe side—her mother's side of the family—she had permitted Charlie Merrett to kiss her. She had felt nothing. She had known Charlie most of her life and he had kissed her on the lips, and she had felt nothing. Sayre Baxendale had merely kissed her on the cheek and she had gone haywire inside. Oh, stop thinking about it, do!

Astra was dressed in a short-sleeved ankle-length dress of deep blue when Greville knocked on her door to see if she was ready to go down. She had dressed her hair up as usual, but tonight wore it in a sophisticated knot on top of her head. She had debated whether to wear her pearl choker, and decided against it, leaving the long column of her throat unadorned.

'How do you do it?' Greville asked when she opened the door.

'Do what?'

'Unfailingly, you always look good enough to eat.'

Had he suspected she was feeling just a smidgen on edge? Whatever, his comments worked. Astra smiled. 'It's a wonder some good woman hasn't snapped you up ages ago,' she laughingly told him as she left her room and they walked along the long landing.

'There's only one woman I'm interested in,' he answered as they headed down the stairs.

He sounded strained somehow, his tone solemn, so unlike him that all her sensitivities went out to him. 'Seriously interested?' she asked as they carried on walking down the wide staircase, knowing he could only be talking of Ellen Morton.

They were at the bottom before he answered. 'I'm going to marry her,' he said quietly.

They were in the hall. Soon they would be with other people. Astra halted, and Greville halted with her. 'Does Ellen know?' she asked gently.

'Not yet,' he answered.

'But she will?'

'Sooner or later. I'd much rather it was sooner, like yesterday. But I'll wait if I have to.'

'Oh, love,' Astra whispered, 'I do hope everything goes well for you.' On impulse, she put her arms around him and gave him a hug and a kiss—she couldn't bear that he might be in agonies while he waited for his love.

'I did get it right?' enquired a voice behind her that she would know anywhere. She took her arms from around Greville and turned to see Sayre Baxendale had emerged from one of the downstairs rooms, and had walked up to them. 'You two *are* cousins?' For all his tone was pleasant enough, Astra didn't miss that there was a hard glint in his eyes. Something had upset him. Good!

'Half cousins, actually,' she answered sunnily, and, glancing at Greville, saw the reason why he hadn't answered for her was that Ellen had just come out into the hall, too. Clearly no one else existed when Ellen was about. Astra flicked her glance back to Sayre. 'But—' she smiled sweetly '—as I mentioned, we're very close.'

Sayre grunted and strode on. Greville remembered he was escorting Astra and, with a hand beneath her elbow, he urged her forward to where Ellen was. 'I couldn't remember if I'd said what time…' Ellen began, and strolled with them to the dining room where it appeared almost everybody had arrived.

A latecomer, and the last to arrive, was Paul Caldwell. A man in his thirties, who no sooner had he taken his bag to his room than he came down, glanced no further than Astra and, regardless that seats at either side of her at the table were taken, pulled up another chair, introduced himself and engagingly opined, 'I refuse to believe you're a friend of Sayre's.' He was right about that, 'He'd never let you out of his sight.'

Astra wasn't much into being engaged by Paul Caldwell. What she was, though, apart from in exceptional circumstances, was well mannered. She was a guest here—and *he*, Sayre, her non-friend, thought her snooty.

She smiled. 'You've obviously been working late. Have you had a chance of anything to eat?' She had taken the subject away from herself, but, on flicking her look past Paul Caldwell, she met Sayre Baxendale's flinty look full-on. For a moment she was at a loss to know what the flinty look was all about. Then it dawned on her that, for all the last time she'd looked Sayre's way he'd seemed to be extraordinarily chummy with the glamorous female sitting next to him—Maxine Hallam, if Astra had remembered the introduction correctly—he must have overheard her comments to Paul Caldwell and, on his sister's behalf, had taken exception to a guest playing the hostess. She could not, Astra felt, do a thing right. If she wasn't being snooty, she was usurping.

She felt very inclined to go up to bed—and stay there until it was time to leave on Sunday morning. 'So why haven't I met you before?' Paul Caldwell, clearly uninterested in food, put his hand on the back of her chair and enquired.

Oh, grief. Astra was saved having to make a reply when Greville leaned across the table. 'How are things in the City, Paul?' he enquired pleasantly.

'Fine,' Paul answered, not too interested in talking shop, apparently, for he turned back to address some other remark to Astra, only Greville addressed her first.

'Did you leave my map in the car, Astra?' he asked, and Astra didn't have to wonder why all three cousins thought the world of him. Extra special though Ellen Morton was to him—she seated on one side of him, with another guest, Ritchie Saunders, seated on the other side—Greville was, as ever, instinctively protective of his half cousin.

Before Astra could reply, however, Paul Caldwell was doing a double take, and enquiring, hurt, 'You and Greville Alford are together?'

She opened her mouth—Sayre Baxendale this time answered for her. 'They're very close,' he informed Paul pleasantly.

Why did she want to laugh? She looked at Sayre, felt her heartbeats doing a funny little skip and felt breathless. She pulled herself together, realising that Sayre Baxendale was of a type she hadn't come across before. Certainly no man she was ever acquainted with had previously had the power to make her insides churn, or to panic her so. Or, for that matter, to make her as angry as he could. She realised then that here was a man who would be dangerous to know.

Good grief! As if she was interested in knowing him any better than she already did. She flicked her gaze away from him. No, thank you very much. The glamorous Maxine was all but drooling over him. She was welcome to him.

Everyone later drifted to the drawing room with talk becoming general. Kit and Vanessa Lister, whom Astra had met at the theatre, were also guests and, finding herself seated next to Vanessa, Astra chatted with her for some while. Vanessa was looking forward tremendously to the point-to-point tomorrow, Astra learned, and they had just started a discussion on horses when, glancing at her cousin, Astra saw that Greville had somehow managed to again be seated next to Ellen.

Astra saw him bend and say something to her, saw Ellen smile, and then heard her laugh, a lovely tinkly sound.

Without being conscious of it, Astra glanced around until she found Sayre. But he was staring at his sister as if it had been a long time since he had heard Ellen laugh so spontaneously.

Suddenly, though, his eyes weren't on Ellen. As if aware someone was watching him, he switched his glance and straight away found Astra. Their eyes met, and held. And Astra's heart went bump. Sayre smiled at her, a slow, devastating smile, and her heart did a double bump. Dangerous to know, screamed a warning in her head—and Astra turned her head away.

'We'll have to start out soon after breakfast,' Vanessa was saying.

I don't want to go, Astra realised all at once—and knew she was panicking again, though hardly knew why. Good heavens, she wasn't afraid of Sayre Baxendale. In fact she wasn't *anything* of Baxendale. She could take him or leave him.

Ten minutes later she happened to glance his way again. Chummy, chummy, chummy, she observed as Maxine Hallam put a hand on Sayre's sleeve to make some comment or other. Astra noticed he didn't seem to mind the glamorous blonde pawing him.

No accounting for tastes, she thought sniffily—and then wondered, good heavens, what was the matter with her? She just didn't *think* like that! It wasn't *her!* Heavens above, anybody would think she was jealous. Jealous! Saints preserve us—it must be time for bed.

Astra did not hang about when the first mutterings of retiring were mooted. Greville was near by then, and Astra told him in an undertone that she was going to bed. 'You don't need me to stay down, do you?' she asked.

'You're not having a good time?'

'Dope. I'm having a fabulous time,' she answered, with a smile.

But, up in her room a short while later, there wasn't a smile about her. She wished that she hadn't come. She wanted to leave, to go home. She wanted to feel safe, and... Safe? Where on earth had that notion come from? Of course she was safe. What could possibly harm her?

Her bed was the last word in comfort—so why couldn't she sleep? After a restless night Astra was up early, showering and shampooing her hair. She dressed in tailored trousers and a white shirt—she'd add a light wool sweater to go to the point-to-point. Only she still didn't particularly feel like going to see horses and riders going like blazes in a steeplechase. She felt out of sorts and much more like being on her own.

There were ten of them staying at Abberley, Astra realised when she entered the breakfast room. Though the first person she clapped eyes on was her host. 'Good morning, Astra,' he greeted her, adding charmingly, 'I don't need to ask how you slept.' *I look a wreck?* 'You're as wide-eyed and beautiful as ever.'

'You've obviously had a refill of charm overnight,' she responded lightly, denying that her insides had gone all melty for a moment.

Ellen came over and asked if she would like a cooked breakfast, but Astra settled for cereal and fruit and sat by her cousin who smilingly informed her, 'I wondered about tapping on your door as I passed, but thought you might be having an extra five minutes.'

Paul Caldwell, coming into the breakfast room and making a bee-line for Astra, stifled any reply she might have made as he complained, 'You didn't tell me that Greville here is your cousin.'

'Didn't I?' she parried politely, as in company she felt that she must.

'Think of it, if I hadn't thought to mention to Kit Lister that it wasn't fair that Greville had hogged the redhead, I'd never have known.' Imagine! And thank you, Kit.

'I'm sure you'd have survived,' Astra answered, becoming aware that Sayre was looking in their direction and was tuned in to their conversation.

'I'll survive better if you'll come with me to the point-to-point.'

Astra didn't care a bit for the way the conversation was going. 'We're all going.' She was determined, as a good guest should be, to stay polite.

'I meant in my car.'

'I'd—rather not,' she answered evenly.

'You'd prefer to go with your cousin?' He obviously didn't believe it. 'Surely you're not that conventional that…'

'Knock it off, Paul,' Greville came in pleasantly. 'Astra goes with me.'

Paul Caldwell looked at him as if he might argue. Then

he turned and smiled at Astra, and, plainly confident of his own charms, said, 'I can see I shall just have to insist you sit with me at lunch.'

Astra smiled back. He could insist all he liked. She had just decided she was not going to go. Were they not both house-guests at Abberley, she might have bluntly told him she wasn't interested. But she had no wish to make any of the other guests feel uncomfortable. But then neither did she want to spend the rest of the day fending off what she was sure would be Paul Caldwell's flirtatious remarks.

When a general move was made to collect sweaters et cetera after breakfast, Astra took the chance for a quiet word with Greville to say she wouldn't be going, but didn't want to draw attention to her decision.

'Paul Caldwell?' Greville queried. How well he knew her.

'It's not just Paul,' she quickly assured him. 'And I'm quite happy—it's just—I don't feel very point-to-pointish right now.'

'I'll stay with you,' Greville stated.

'Greville Alford!' she exclaimed, knowing where his heart lay. 'As if I'd let you!'

They were both laughing as Sayre Baxendale came by. Without a word he passed them and, while that didn't appear to bother her cousin in any degree, Astra owned to feeling a bit fluttery. Nonsense!

'You're sure you'll be all right?'

'Of course I will!' she told him stoutly.

'I'll have a quiet word with Sayre and let him know that we'll be one short in the party.'

Astra at once wanted to protest, but since Sayre couldn't be bothered to say a word just now she had an idea he'd be highly delighted not to have her company. After all, he'd seen his sister smiling and laughing, and that was what this

weekend was all about—Ellen getting into the swim of
things again, and being happy.

Astra went up to her room and stayed there while cars
were brought round to the front drive. She kept away from
the windows and waited a while, only going to look out
when the last car turned out of the drive.

It was going to be a fine, warm day. Five minutes later,
deciding she wouldn't require a sweater, Astra left her
room. Abberley was set in acres and acres of grounds. She
headed past the beautiful gardens and towards the trees and
fields.

Half an hour later and she was truly beginning to enjoy
herself. Her decision to not go to the point-to-point had
been the right one. It seemed an absolute age since she had
taken herself off for a long walk. She had forgotten the
pleasure to be found in just striding along, watching birds,
observing bees busy at the occasional crop of late wild
flowers, coming across the odd rabbit here and there before
it hastened away.

She thought of many things. About how absolutely wonderful it was that both Yancie and Fennia had found such
happiness. Oh, what a relief it had been to both of them
that the Jolliffe gene had not been passed down to them.
Astra knew, though, that she could not afford to relax her
guard. Their certainty that they were not, and would never
be, like their loose-moralled mothers stemmed from Yancie
falling in love with Thomson and Fennia falling in love
with Jegar. Both her cousins had assured her that once you
fell in love it was truly inconceivable that you would let
any other man take you in his arms, much less that you
should want to be in any man's arms other than those of
the man you loved.

Astra remained to be convinced. She had no intention of
falling in love, and certainly had no intention of having any
man's arms around her. By no manner or means was she

going to be like her mother—who, to date, was seldom without some man's arms around her.

More and more determined that she was not going to be like her mother, Astra strode on as if striding to outstep the fear that she might turn out to be as promiscuous as Imogen. Logic tried to tell her that if she was going to be fast and loose like her parent it would have shown itself before now. But Astra was not going to take any chances.

Suddenly she was remembering Sayre Baxendale's kiss to her cheek yesterday. She remembered that tingling sensation that... Oh, for goodness' sake!

Realising she had been out some while and had walked many miles, Astra thought that perhaps she ought to be making her way back. She turned about.

She wished, though, that she had never let Sayre Baxendale into her thoughts, for now she didn't seem to be able to get him out of them. She supposed she had been trying to avoid thinking about him ever since she had left the house. But it was as if, having at last let him in, he was now refusing to budge from her thoughts.

Odious creature. With a bit of luck she would just have to suffer him at dinner tonight, possibly breakfast tomorrow morning and then Greville would drive her home and she would never have to see S. Baxendale esquire ever again.

Well, she qualified, should her half cousin have his heart's desire and get Ellen to agree to marry him—and heaven alone knew how far into the future that would be— she would put up with seeing Baxendale at the wedding. Though, if the clinging Maxine Hallam had her way, Baxendale would probably be married himself by then— and serve him right. Somehow, and she didn't know why, but to Astra's mind Maxine Hallam wasn't right for Sayre.

Pfff, as if she cared! Astra strode on, and found she was growing niggled. And why wouldn't she? How dared he call her snooty? He could talk with his 'haughty beyond the point of arrogance'. It was too much. Add that to the 'North Pole Northcott' that had apparently reached Baxendale's ears, and she was starting to feel just a bit fed up with the labels being pinned on her. Even Paul Caldwell was at it. Even he had been ready to label her 'conventional'. By that did he mean staid?

Astra was not at all happy with her thoughts when, walking down the side of a hedgerow a short way from the house, she came to a wooden stile she had previously negotiated by use of its steps.

Snooty, staid, North Pole Northcott, all jumbled together in her head. *Cool and aloof, haughty beyond the point of arrogance.* Huh! To hear them talk—male every one— you'd think that she never ever let her hair down.

Rebellion, defiance against all labels struck just as she was about to step on to the stile. To blazes with it! Without thinking further she took five paces back—and took a run at the stile. She should, she soon learned, have taken ten paces back and built up more impetus. Because, instead of sailing clear over the stile, she clipped the top with the toe of her shoe and, instead of the elegant landing she anticipated, she fell awkwardly in a very ungainly heap.

She sat up—and dumbfoundedly, before she had a hope of getting herself together, heard someone applauding! Having been positive that there couldn't possibly be another soul around, Astra jerked her head up and, to her utmost chagrin, saw Sayre Baxendale standing there saluting her performance. Where had he sprung from?

'Your triple salchow very nearly came off,' he drawled, amusement in every word.

She hated him. 'I could have killed myself!' she hurled at him nastily.

'I saw you move—you didn't look dead,' he observed pleasantly.

Her ankle hurt—so did her loss of dignity. 'Goodbye,' she said—and found he wasn't so easily dismissed.

'What sort of bounder do you think I am?' he drawled, coming over to her, but amusement still there. 'Do let me help you up.'

She was in pain; she wanted to hit him. She gave him a peeved look, but when he extended a hand ready to pull her up she realised she had no choice and stretched up a hand to meet his.

He hoisted, she put force on her good foot—but it was no good. A cry of pain escaped when she put pressure on her injured foot and she collapsed against him.

She held on to him—something he seemed to understand she would never do in normal circumstances. For, holding her firmly, he pulled back to look into her face. 'You're hurt!' There wasn't a shred of amusement about him now. 'Where?' he demanded.

There was just no way she could refuse to answer or tell him to clear off—much as she would have liked to do. 'My ankle—the right one,' she answered.

Sayre helped her to the stile and sat her down and examined her right ankle. 'Trust you to twist your ankle a quarter of a mile away from civilisation.'

'Help me stand!' she ordered, annoyed with him, cross with herself, but glad to accept his diagnosis of a twisted ankle, for all it felt painful enough to be a break.

'Where were you thinking of going?'

Sarcastic swine. 'I'm not asking you to carry me!' she told him snootily, and didn't care a button that she did sound snooty.

'I'm glad about that—you look a bit hefty to me.' He straight away cut her down to size.

The swine! The utter swine! 'I'm as slender as the proverbial reed!' she defended hotly. 'And why aren't you at the point-to-point?' she demanded.

He looked down at her; her normally pale face was flushed—with embarrassment as well as anger—and he smiled. 'Something seemed to be telling me my services would be needed here,' he answered. And, looking at her, he seemed to be considering his options, before proclaiming, 'Come on, little Astra, let's get you home.'

For several seconds she waited to know how this was going to be achieved. By no stretch of the imagination was she going to be able to walk, or even hop the four hundred or so yards to the house. Then Sayre reached down and, as if she were a featherweight, he put her to stand on the stile step with her good foot, and promptly turned his back and came close up.

'One leg at a time,' he suggested, and Astra knew he intended to piggy-back her to the house.

'Can't you go and get a tractor or something?' she protested, not moving, not looking forward at all to being carted back to the house like a sack of potatoes.

'It will be quicker this way,' he answered, and, putting his arms back, he reached for her.

Astra felt a clown as they set off. She supposed Baxendale was right and that for him to walk back to the house and then ring round trying to find a farmer with a tractor sitting idle might take some while.

'Why haven't you got a mobile phone like everyone else?' she complained, her injured foot stuck out but every movement jarring. She was not at her sunniest.

'Why haven't you?' he countered, and she knew, damn him, that he was right. She hadn't thought to bring her mobile when she'd come out for a walk—why would she need it? No more had he.

Her dignity began to hurt as much as her foot. Fat chance she'd got of maintaining a cool exterior now. So much for being snooty! She was sure she must look as ridiculous as she felt—haughty beyond the point of arrogance? It looked like it.

'You're loving this, aren't you?' she accused, stifling a cry of pain as her foot received another jar.

She clutched at him and her breasts bumped against his back. 'I'm finding it quite—um—pleasurable,' he answered cheerfully.

Her face flamed. 'I didn't mean *that!* Put me down at once!' she commanded. The house was in sight; she'd crawl on her hands and knees if she had to.

Her command was ignored. 'Do shut up, Astra.' He added insult to injury. She was a professional woman, or had been—until he'd wrecked her career. How dared he tell her to shut up? The back of his head was so inviting, she would have loved to give it a punch.

'Swine!' she hissed, and half expected him to dump her there and then. But, to her surprise, he burst out laughing.

'Oh, Astra, Astra,' he said softly. 'Don't make me laugh—I need all the breath I can find.'

Instantly, she was contrite. He could have left her back at that stile to wait what might have proved an absolutely age for him to run some sort of conveyance to earth. 'I'm sorry,' she mumbled.

She stayed silent for the rest of the way back to the house. Once there, 'Stand on your good foot while I open the door,' he ordered, setting her down.

'I can make it to my room by myself now,' she informed him, striving with all she had not to wince as she hobbled through the door and Sayre closed it.

He gave her a disgusted look, and she just knew he had added stubborn to his other list of names he had for her. But, before she had a chance to utter a word of protest, he scooped her up in his arms and—as if she weighed nothing—he was carrying her up the stairs.

She was hating him again, with a vengeance, by the time

he had carried her into her room. He sat her on her bed and raised her injured foot to inspect it again. Astra inspected it too, and just could not believe that in so short a time her normally narrow and slender foot had swollen to over twice its size.

When Sayre went to remove her shoe, however, she protested, 'Don't do that!' He still had a gentle hold of her foot, but glanced up. 'I'll never get my shoe on again if you take it off,' she informed him.

'You've ideas of going somewhere?'

'I can't stay here being a nuisance.'

'Who says you can't?'

So he *did* think she'd be a nuisance. That was soon remedied. 'You wouldn't care to drive me to my apartment, I suppose?' she suggested prettily.

He smiled, and she knew the answer was no, before he drawled, 'What? And be left worrying about you because there's no one there to look after you?'

'As if,' she jeered, 'prettily' soon dumped.

'Besides,' he went on reasonably, 'Paul Caldwell will be devastated if, having missed sitting with you at lunch, he has to miss you not being around for dinner either.'

There was no answer to that, other than a speaking look. Sayre took her silence for her having been stumped, and carried on with what he had always intended anyway. He removed not one shoe but, while he was at it, the other one as well.

Then, to her outright astonishment, 'You'd better take your trousers off,' he said matter-of-factly. Astra stared at him, her green eyes growing wider and wider. Sayre glanced at her, his glance momentarily arrested. Then, moving closer, his hands went to the waistband of her trousers. 'You want me to do it,' he began, as if understanding that every movement hurt.

'No!' Astra shrieked, panicking like she'd never panicked before, knocking his hands furiously away, her face scarlet.

Sayre pulled back, staring at her. 'Oh, my...' he began. Then, rapidly recovering, a smile—that devastating smile— broke and he said, 'It's true, isn't it, little Astra?' And, while she stared hostilely at him, he added, 'No man has ever touched you?'

'That's got absolutely nothing to do with you!' she flared angrily, feeling again that she would quite enjoy hitting him.

'Because you're frigid?'

My stars, did he never let go? 'Go to hell!' she flew— and hoped she'd offended him for life and that he threw her out—she'd go home by taxi.

But she hadn't offended him, it seemed. And his tone was gently persuasive when he crooned, 'Poor Astra, you're hurting like the blazes, and I'm the only one around to take it out on.'

'Who better?' she snapped.

He smiled. 'All I want is for you to be comfortable,' he stated, adding practically, 'Believe me, if that foot swells up any more, short of slitting the seams, you won't be able to get your trousers off at all.' She hadn't thought of that. 'I'd get Mrs Turner, my housekeeper, or one of her assistants up here to help you, but they're all up to their eyes in other work.'

'I don't need help,' Astra retorted, fully understanding that with all these extra people staying this weekend, even with additional help, Mrs Turner the housekeeper had more than enough to do without leaving everything to come and help her out of her trousers. 'Thank you for getting me this far,' she managed, kill her though it did. 'I can cope fine now,' she added nicely. And, when he just stood there looking at her, 'So clear off,' she ordered bluntly.

He laughed, in fact went off laughing, and, left to herself,

Astra felt that she did not hate him after all. In fact, she quite liked him. Thank goodness he was such a fit specimen. He'd carried her all of a quarter of a mile.

Her aching ankle took her mind off Sayre for a while. It did, however, seem a good idea of his for her to get out of her trousers, though that was easier said than done. It was a struggle but, feeling hot, bothered and not a little exhausted, Astra eventually inched her trouser leg over her injured foot.

She all at once felt as though she ached all over. She felt weepy too suddenly—but wouldn't weep. Grateful that her silk robe was at the foot of the bed, she shrugged out of her shirt, donned the robe and decided to try and sleep.

Astra pulled the bedcover down, and, prior to trying to sleep, took the securing hairpins from her chignon. Her rich red hair cascaded about her shoulders; she plumped up her pillows. She felt exhausted, but not sleepy.

She was about to lie down and try to rest, anyway, when suddenly her bedroom door opened and, bearing a tray, beneath which, she observed, was a plastic bowl, Sayre Baxendale came in.

Astra was shaken to see him so unexpectedly, but, as Sayre closed the door and came close up to the bed, so he seemed to be a touch staggered. 'Beautiful,' he observed softly, 'is an understatement,' his eyes on her face, her hair.

'I...' she said helplessly. 'I didn't expect you to come back!' And Sayre seemed to rapidly recover.

Though his tone was still quiet, gentle, when he said, 'Poor love, sitting there like that, with your fantastic hair framing your face; you look totally vulnerable.'

It was pretty much how she felt. 'I don't—know what to do,' she mumbled, wondering where the dickens her normal backbone had gone.

At that, Sayre took charge. He smiled. 'First of all, you take these painkillers,' he began.

'You're a gent,' she sighed gratefully.

'Then, after you've tackled the chicken salad I've scrounged from the kitchen, you can have a nice long rest until dinner.'

Astra wasn't sure how she felt about being bossed around. She wasn't used to it; it went against the grain. But she was grateful for the couple of tablets he handed her and the glass of water he'd thought to bring for her to wash them down.

Having downed the tablets, knowing that relief from the pain wouldn't be very far away, a large chunk of backbone reasserted itself. She was glad it was so. All she had on under her thin wrap were her bra and briefs, and she was starting to feel very awkward with the all-male Sayre Baxendale staring down at her. It didn't help that her hair was about her shoulders—what chance of maintaining a cool and aloof front now, looking as she must?

'What's with the bowl?' she rallied to enquire belligerently, indicating the plastic bowl he had brought in with him.

She saw him eye her sharply. But he had an antidote for her belligerence, she soon realised, when he smiled nicely, and answered, 'I've looked it up—the best treatment for a swollen ankle is to plunge it into ice cold water.'

'You'd love that, wouldn't you?' she challenged, not believing for a moment that he'd read that anywhere. Though he might, she conceded, while he went to the bathroom to put some cold water in the bowl, have learned that from his housekeeper.

Sayre returned with the bowl and with a large towel tucked under an arm. 'Come on, Astra,' he encouraged, placing the bowl down by the side of the bed. 'Time to dunk your tootsie.'

She wanted to laugh, but told herself that, while he was only trying to make her feel better by being light-hearted, she was in no mood for light-hearted. 'You go, I'll manage,' she insisted.

He looked at her and grinned. 'I couldn't possibly let you,' he insisted.

Damn him. She edged to the side of her bed, her face growing scarlet as her robe dragged beneath her and parted so that not only were her legs on view, but half of her thighs as well.

'I can't...' she gasped, struggling to cover herself up.

Sayre transferred his glance from her silken thighs to her scarlet face, his expression friendly, no more than that. 'Yes, you can,' he contradicted her lightly, and in the next moment he had shaken out the large towel and had draped it over her, hiding her thighs from view. Though he had not, by any stretch of the imagination, forgotten what his eyes had seen when, taking a hold of her right leg by the calf and guiding it into the water, 'I know it's against all you believe to let any man get this close,' he chatted away matter-of-factly. 'So, in case no one else has dared...' he broke off to glance up at her as he gently stroked her foot into the water '...may I be the first to state you have the most fabulous legs?'

'That's it!' she snapped. 'I don't need you or this water!' With that she went to jerk her foot out of the bowl. It was a mistake. It hurt like billy-o. She could not hold in a small cry of pain.

'That's what you get for being bad-tempered,' Sayre Baxendale mocked—and how she kept herself from hitting him then she just didn't know. 'Gently, gently,' he murmured, and as though to soothe her he carefully placed her swollen foot back in the bowl and while she let it stay there he tenderly stroked her calf.

Just when she began to relax, Astra didn't know. What she did know, suddenly—and totally staggeringly—was that the way Sayre was caressing her leg was not unpleasant. In fact, her whole body seemed to be tingling from just his touch and she was quite enjoying...*caressing!* Astra came to, with a start.

'Stop doing that!' she ordered—and was as appalled as Sayre seemed surprised by the husky note in her voice.

His hand stilled and he glanced at her. Then suddenly he was grinning—quite wickedly. 'Well!' he exclaimed. 'Who would have thought it?' She tried to head him off, knowing she was not going to like it, whatever it was he was about to add—and, looking at him, she just knew he was going to add something—but her voice failed her completely, and she had to sit and suffer as he completed, 'I do believe the frigid little virgin has come over all—er-peculiar.'

That was the time she should have hit him. But she was much more interested in furiously denying that Baxendale's stroking her leg had had any effect on her at all.

'Don't be so inane!' she raged angrily, loudly—even in her own ears it sounding as if she was protesting too much.

He obviously thought so too, because he didn't answer but, clearly thinking her 'tootsie' had been dunked enough, he removed it from the bowl, took the covering towel from her and matter-of-factly dried her foot. While he went to the bathroom to empty the bowl, Astra made rapid efforts to get herself decently covered up. She was sitting in the middle of the bed, her robe back in place, when he returned.

'I'll bandage...'

'That won't be necessary,' Astra told him coolly, and had to suffer his long, considering stare for long moments.

Then he was coming over and sitting beside her on the edge of the bed. She was glad it was a double one. For all he was close, at least there was a little distance between them. Astonishingly, though, he reached over and caught hold of her had. 'You know, Astra, there's nothing wrong in having feelings,' he assured her gently.

'I don't need a lecture!' she told him arrogantly.

She had hoped her arrogance would see him striding from her room, but he didn't seem a scrap bothered by it. 'Who did this to you?' he startled her by asking.

'Did what?' she answered—when she hadn't been going to say a word.

'Made you all frozen up inside—afraid of your emotions.'

'Don't be absurd!'

'Was it some man?'

'Huh!' she scorned, and was shaken to the core by the way he looked first furious and then quite unbelievably gentle.

'Oh, sweetheart,' he breathed, 'were you—attacked? Did some...?'

'No, I was not!' she flared. Honestly! 'For goodness' sake—there's nothing the matter with me!' Sayre just sat and silently looked at her—his very silence forcing her on. 'You're imagining a problem that simply isn't there,' she fumed. Still he was silent. 'I don't know what type of woman you usually go around with.' Well, yes, she did, actually. Astra didn't feel any better for remembering the glamorous Maxine Hallam. 'B-but not all w-women are...' Astra couldn't finish, and sent him a seething look of dislike.

Sayre smiled, a gentle smile. 'When was the last time you were kissed?' he enquired kindly. Then, as if remembering that he had kissed her only last evening when she arrived, 'On the mouth,' he qualified.

She smiled back insincerely. 'If you're trying to suggest that I've never been kissed, then I'm afraid I shall have to disillusion you. Charles Merrett and I...'

'Were never lovers,' Sayre cut in as though he knew it for a fact.

'Maybe not,' she had to concede, but damned if she was

going to let the side down. 'But I assure you I'm perfectly normal.'

Sayre smiled again. 'Isn't that what started this fascinating discussion? My suggestion that you were?'

She, Astra fumed, had had just about enough of him. 'Oh, clear off!' she told him angrily, and didn't like at all the still, thoughtful look of him.

'I will—if you kiss me goodbye,' he had the audacity to reply.

'Get lost!'

'You're scared.'

'No, I'm not.'

'Yes, you are.'

'It's not my habit to go around kissing every Tom, Dick or Harry.'

'I know that. But my name's Sayre, and I've just carried you miles,' he exaggerated. 'And I deserve a kiss for my trouble.' She eyed him antagonistically. He squeezed her hand. 'I won't harm you,' he promised softly.

Astra lay back amongst the pillows and closed her eyes. Perhaps if she lay perfectly still he'd get the message and go. Half a minute ticked by. She started to feel a little panicky and wanted desperately to open her eyes—but stubbornly wouldn't. 'Shut the door on your way out,' she told him jerkily.

She felt the bed move—and thought he was leaving. But it went down again—and her eyes flew open to see he hadn't left the bed, but had moved further on to it—moved nearer.

'What...?' she gasped.

He bent over her. 'If you'd just close your eyes for another second, I could give you that kiss goodbye,' he murmured softly.

No way was she going to close her eyes now. Astra stared at him, fighting a battle of wanting him gone, of not wanting him to kiss her, but having a sinking feeling that she couldn't have both. She swallowed hard. Took a deep breath. 'One second, that's all!' she snappily gave in, and closed her eyes. For an agonising five seconds, nothing happened.

Then Astra felt Sayre get closer, felt him lean over her, his chest touching her. She started to tremble and then felt his mouth against her own in a gentle kiss.

She couldn't breathe; her eyes flew wide. Sayre was looking down at her. 'Hey, it's okay,' he soothed, sounding concerned as her trembling communicated itself to him. 'I'll go,' he said. But checked. 'I can't leave you like this.'

'I'm fine,' she replied huskily, finding her voice, and, with unsought intelligence, all at once realising that she could trust him and that, as he promised, he wouldn't harm her.

Sayre looked doubtful. 'You're sure?'

'Positive,' she answered.

'You're still shaking.'

He seemed worried and, most oddly, considering not too long ago she had felt angry enough with him to want to punch his head, Astra found she didn't want him to be. Involuntarily she raised a hand and touched his shoulder as if seeking a way to assure him that he had nothing to worry about.

'You can kiss me again, if you want.' Had she just said that? She wanted at once to retract the words, but the concerned look was starting to leave Sayre. And he smiled.

'Close your eyes,' he murmured.

She didn't—until his head came down, and he gently placed his mouth over hers. She was trembling again, and hadn't realised when her trembling had previously stopped. But as his mouth tenderly lingered on hers her whole body began to tingle as though electrified. She felt anxious then that, should Sayre feel her trembling, he might again grow concerned—and break that kiss.

Shyly she raised her other hand and held his other shoulder. Sayre broke his whisper of a kiss and pulled back to look into her eyes. And he smiled again, reassuring her this time as he teased, 'At the risk of seeming greedy, may I have another?'

She laughed; she couldn't help it. A light, giving laugh. It was all the answer Sayre needed. His head came nearer and, tenderly again, he kissed her. Astra, kissed him back.

Again he pulled back, and she smiled up at him. Sayre bent his head and gently kissed the side of her neck. Then once more his lips claimed hers. Only this time his kiss was deeper—and Astra did not back away from it. Something was happening to her, something which she seemed powerless to stop. Something which she didn't want to stop. She *wanted* to explore kissing with him.

When Sayre took her in his arms and held her close, Astra shyly put her arms around him. The tip of his tongue touched her bottom lip—and she pulled back with a gasp.

'Sorry,' she apologised at once. 'I—er...'

'I'm sorry,' he cut in gently, making her smile. 'I forgot your rookie status, and got a little carried away.'

'Is it all right to kiss like this? The way we are?' she asked, her sophisticated image in shreds about her.

'Does it feel all right?'

She searched for words to tell him she enjoyed exploring kissing with him. But didn't want him to think her totally naïve, so said simply, 'Yes,' and was rewarded by a deep and lingering kiss.

For many long minutes they lay together gently kissing, and then something was changing. Sayre's kisses were growing deeper and deeper. He kissed her throat and her eyes and she had never experienced such wonderful sensations as he aroused in her.

Though when she felt his hand caress inside the neck of her robe she wasn't at all sure how she felt about that. His hand moved to her shoulder, its heat scorching as he moved her bra strap down her arm.

'I...' she choked blindly, a riot of emotions shooting through her as he tenderly caressed her shoulder.

'You?' Sayre looked at her to enquire.

'I—d-don't think I want you to do that.'

'You don't sound too sure,' he teased, still doing it. 'Don't you like it?'

She swallowed. 'Yes, but...'

'But...'

'Well—it's—er—a bit—personal.'

Sayre stared at her as if he just could not believe his ears, then that devastating smile of his flashed out, and he laughed softly. 'Oh, Astra, sweetheart—you don't think this, you and I on your bed together, embracing, kissing, is not just a *bit* personal?' Astra went a touch pink, and, seeing he had embarrassed her, Sayre murmured, 'Sweetheart, you're wonderful,' and proceeded to kiss her embarrassment away.

Passion started to soar, and she had no objection at all to make when Sayre pushed her robe from her shoulder and kissed and caressed her, trailing kisses across from her shoulder to her throat. He moved closer to her, and Astra, feeling his body against her, began to feel all shy again— and not a little hot and bothered—yet at the same time unable to deny Sayre had triggered off in her desires undreamed of!

She made a jerky movement, although she was entirely unsure what she intended to do. But then it was, perhaps Sayre having taken care to keep his feet away from her injured foot, that she caught her right foot against him— and the pain was excruciating.

'Oh!' she gasped, and it was very plain that it was not

a cry of passion. Astra knew then that, their lovemaking having been an excellent antidote for pain, that antidote was no longer working.

Astra stared at him; there had seemed something special about his arms around her. She opened her mouth but was scared she might say as much, and found, when looking for something alternative to say, that his heady kisses seemed to have scrambled her brain. 'Was that making love?' she asked—and wanted to die at the idiocy of it.

But Sayre didn't scoff at her as she had supposed he might. Instead he bent and buried his face in the deep richness of her thick red hair, before placing another kiss to the side of her neck, and, signalling that her exploration into kissing was over, he drew away from her back to the edge of the bed. 'You're sensational,' he smiled, and, his smile gently deepening, 'That was making love,' he agreed, though amended after a moment, 'Well, skirting the perimeters.' He tapped her nose. 'Though how you've managed to stay outside those perimeters this long, without some male taking you inside their boundaries, defeats me.'

'What do you mean?' Astra asked, striving for brain power—she wanted him to kiss her again, wanted to lie with him.

'You had me going for a while there, Astra,' he admitted. 'I was almost in danger of forgetting you are my guest.'

Astra began to doubt her sanity. She actually felt *glad* she'd had him going for a while there. Good heavens, what on earth was she thinking about? 'You don't normally seduce your guests?' she enquired, her tone husky still, but more controlled than it had been.

Sayre grinned a wicked grin, and Astra had an idea she could forget cool and aloof, forget haughty. Sayre had seen through her cover to the more soft and vulnerable person she truly was. 'Not unless they've been specially invited for that purpose,' he assured her.

Astra's emotions had taken a severe, if pleasant, battering one way and another. But, while she admitted to be feeling more than a degree or two confused by everything that had happened in this last half hour or so, she knew that for the first time in her life she wanted a member of the opposite sex to think her attractive.

'You—don't fancy me?' she just had to ask.

'Ye gods—you're even more innocent than I thought!' Sayre exclaimed. 'Either that or you've a very short memory.'

Astra stared at him. 'You mean—just now?'

'Of course I mean just now.'

'But you didn't—we didn't...'

'We didn't,' he agreed.

'Why not?' Where did these dreadful questions keep coming from? It was as if, her curiosity about such matters suddenly kicked into life, that curiosity just wouldn't stay down. 'Not that I would have,' she added hastily. 'Not that I wanted to,' she added even more hastily—and wanted once more to hit him when he laughed.

'Of course you didn't,' he agreed, like the gent she had called him. He stood up and slipped on his shoes, which she'd had no idea he'd removed, and told her, 'Think about it.' And while Astra stared at him—think about it? Think of why he hadn't pressed to make complete love to her?—'I'm going—before I do something we may both regret,' he said shortly.

Astra wanted to tell him 'No chance' but she hesitated. Unbelievable as she yesterday would have thought it, if Sayre took her in his arms once more, she wasn't at all sure that she wouldn't end up responding—totally.

'Don't forget your tootsie bowl,' she managed to remind him lightly. And when, without saying another word, he crossed to the door and departed, he went leaving her with a very great deal to think about.

CHAPTER FIVE

ASTRA wished several times during the afternoon that Greville would come back from the point-to-point and each time she felt mean for thinking any such thing. Greville was out with the woman he loved. He deserved every scrap of happiness.

Astra sighed. It was just that Greville represented something secure and solid in her life and, she owned, she felt so concern-ridden just then, so very much all over the place, that she would welcome secure and solid.

It was a fact: Sayre Baxendale's kisses, and her response to those kisses, had rocked her—and she felt quite desperate to be the person she had been before Sayre and his kisses had turned her organised world upside down. Astra had soon put her hair up in a severe knot. But it did not help. The damage was done. Raw anxiety kept her wide awake. Forget that her ankle was hurting. More painful than that were the nightmare thoughts which she just could not keep away—was she, in spite of all her efforts, turning out to be just like her mother?

That horrendous thought was one she couldn't live with. The fact that all those fears and worries of promiscuity she had grown up guarding against had been nowhere in sight once Sayre had begun kissing her—making love with her—was frightening. It was wrong, and yet—it had felt so right.

Both Yancie and Fennia had said it would feel right when she was in the arms of the man she loved. But Astra knew that she didn't love Sayre Baxendale. Did she? Of course she didn't. Why, she didn't even like him half the

97

time. Oh, help her, somebody—she didn't want to be like her mother.

Astra's agonies about the eagerness she had discovered in herself to return Sayre's kisses were momentarily quieted when Mrs Turner sent up one of her assistants with some tea and to remove her barely touched lunch tray.

'Oh, you shouldn't have bothered,' Astra protested, fully aware of how everything must be bustling in the kitchen.

'It's a pleasure,' the young woman smiled, but too soon departed and left Astra to be once more bombarded by her demons.

It was a great relief to hear the point-to-point party returning. By that time it was as though indelibly written—never, ever again was she going to kiss Sayre Baxendale, or allow him to kiss her. Though, recalling Sayre admitting that she'd had him 'going for a while there', and how he hadn't taken it any further but had left her to 'think about' why he hadn't, Astra was still no further in fathoming out why hadn't he?

She guessed he wouldn't attempt to seduce her, his guest, again. Not that he had attempted to seduce her—not that she would let him... Oh, her head ached just trying to puzzle it out. She... Her door opened and Greville came hurrying in.

'Oh, love,' he sympathised, his eyes going from her pale face down to her swollen ankle. 'Sayre said you'd taken a bit of a tumble—but look at you.'

'I'm fine,' she protested, and felt her insides go haywire when Sayre, with Ritchie Saunders close behind him, followed Greville in through the open door.

'How are you feeling?' Sayre asked evenly, his cool dark glance taking in her scorching blush.

Astra bravely tilted her head an arrogant fraction. 'Fine,' she lied, flicking him the briefest glance, her insides playing a game of their own.

His look was sceptical. 'Ritchie wants to take a look at that foot.' *Bring everybody in, why don't you? I just adore being a peep show.*

'Ritchie's a doctor,' Greville, perhaps reading her mutinous expression, chipped in.

'Oh,' Astra murmured, and while Ritchie Saunders came over all Dr Richard Saunders she said, 'Perhaps you'll close the door on the way out.'

'I do believe your patient prefers not to have an audience and is throwing us out,' Sayre drawled to the doctor.

'You're getting to know her,' Greville smiled, and as Sayre stared into Astra's wide green eyes so, humiliatingly, she blushed again.

Richard Saunders examined her ankle as soon as Sayre and Greville had gone. He was pleasant, cheerful and thorough. He it was who bandaged up her foot and told her to keep her weight off it. He it was who dosed her up with more painkillers and told her to try and have a little sleep. Adding, with a smile, 'But don't deprive us of your company at dinner tonight.'

Astra thanked him, but was unsure how she was going to present herself at the dinner table that night *and* keep her weight off her injured foot.

Ellen came in to see Astra almost as soon as the doctor had gone. 'Oh, Astra. What a dreadful thing to happen while you're a guest here at Abberley.'

'It was my own stupid fault,' Astra confessed; the last thing she wanted was that Ellen should feel guilt over it.

'Sayre said you tripped getting over a stile.'

By the sound of it he hadn't revealed she had been doing a bit of unsophisticated vaulting practice. Astra didn't thank him for it—through him she was an inner mass of anxiety. 'It was lucky Sayre was around at the time. How was the point-to-point?' she asked brightly.

Ellen was still with her when ten minutes later Greville

returned, and as Astra looked from one to the other they seemed so right for each other. Ellen's eyes when they rested on Greville seemed to hold a special light in them somehow.

'Would you like me to take you back home?' Greville asked, as somehow Astra had known that he would. But, while she would like nothing better, she couldn't do that to him. Even though she was so churned up inside, she just could not accept what for him would be a great sacrifice. What he wanted was to be here with Ellen—every minute that he could.

'I'd like to stay—if you don't think I'll be a nuisance,' she answered lightly.

'You won't be any trouble at all,' Ellen said quickly, and Astra was sure she heard relief in her tones. 'When you're ready I'll come and help you get dressed, and...'

'And I'll organise a stretcher party to carry you downstairs.' Greville—her one-time sophisticated cousin—almost tripped over his words in his eagerness.

Having pleasantly assured Ellen she could manage on her own, Astra bathed and got ready with some difficulty and was sitting dressed in a long, discreetly fitting dress of deep apricot when she heard her 'stretcher party' arriving. She prayed that Sayre wouldn't be part of it—the very thought of him touching her again made her feel uptight and unable to relax.

She need not have worried. 'See what happens to you when you prefer your own company to mine?' Paul Caldwell joked when, Greville having knocked at her door, the two of them came in. 'You'd have come to far less harm had you not so wickedly devastated me by ducking out of today's shindig and going off on pursuits of your own.'

In complete contrast to the way she had viewed Paul Caldwell previously, Astra now found Paul and his flirtatious but harmless banter a welcome relief from the agitation of her thoughts. She had been agitated at first as to whether Sayre had triggered that wayward gene so that now she would look favourably on any man's attentions. However, with tremendous relief as Greville and Paul 'chaired' her downstairs, she knew that wasn't so. Instinctively she knew that if Paul attempted to kiss her the way Sayre had she would give Paul very short shrift. It therefore followed, she concluded, that if she had inherited that gene then she must be selective in her waywardness. Clearly she wasn't interested in blatantly obvious men.

Not that she was interested in Sayre Baxendale, for goodness' sake! Oh, what a nightmare the whole thing was. She must be on her guard against types like Baxendale, though. For her own peace of mind, she had to be.

Because she had realised that Paul Caldwell was not a problem, Astra felt able to be more friendly with him than she had so far been. Likewise, as if he had decided his brash tactics were getting him nowhere, she found that Paul had toned down his too obvious manner. It was next to Paul that Astra discovered she was sitting at dinner.

And she was glad about that—she told herself. Well, why wouldn't she be glad? He was amusing, he made her laugh—and certainly she didn't want to sit next to Baxendale. Not that he'd have noticed if she had been. Not with chummy Maxine Hallam sitting beside him and hanging on his every word.

Astra gave in to the impulse to flick a glance in Sayre's direction. He was looking at her! Their eyes met. She gave him a cool half smile—he didn't smile at all. She looked away.

'And what sort of work do you do?' Paul, having light-heartedly disclosed something of his business world, wanted to know what she did for a living.

She gave him a full smile, hoped Baxendale was looking—and wondered what in creation she was so peeved about. 'I'm between jobs at the moment,' she answered, determined she wasn't going to be embarrassed if the man who knew precisely why she was between jobs at the moment had his radar scanner tuned into her conversation.

'What kind of job would that be?' Paul insisted.

'Finance,' she answered quietly.

'Really?' He was interested. 'Whom did you work for last? Perhaps I know them.'

She was sure he did. Her reluctance to answer, however, stemmed purely from an intuitive feeling that his follow-up question would be to ask why she did leave.

'I—er...' She delayed. But, realising she was giving his everyday question far too much importance, she told him, 'Um, Yarroll Finance, actually.'

'Yarroll Finance!' Paul exclaimed, impressed. 'You must be good at your job to have worked for them.' And, as expected, he asked, 'Why did you leave?'

Astra felt she had more than enough going on in her head to cope with, without having to dream up some sort of evasive answer that would keep her pride intact. 'I...I—er...' she faltered—and discovered that Sayre must have had his radar scanner tuned in her direction because, incredibly, he seemed more than happy to answer for her!

'I believe I know why you left,' he butted into their conversation. And, because of her injured foot she was incapable of galloping out of the room, she had to sit there while Sayre shamed her in front of the three or four people who now seemed equally interested. 'Didn't I hear you'd been head-hunted by a couple of companies and in fairness to Yarroll's resigned while you considered your options?'

Feeling stunned, Astra simply sat and stared at him. He was neither smiling nor unsmiling. 'S-something like that,' she managed—and was never more glad when he took the attention away from her and addressed Paul.

'Your glass is empty,' he noticed in the manner of the perfect host, and Paul took up his suggestion to refill his glass.

'As I'm not driving,' he accepted, and the man on Astra's other side turned to her and soon they were having a discussion on a recent thriller which it turned out they had both read.

The meal was delicious, but Astra was barely aware of what she had eaten. There was a general move to the drawing room afterwards, and Paul Caldwell and Ritchie Saunders carried her to the drawing room and assisted her on to a sofa. Astra saw Sayre had his eyes on her. He didn't seem too pleased about something but was soon smiling as Maxine Hallam sidled over to him.

Suddenly Astra was feeling all confused again. She would dearly have liked to go straight up to her room. But, having just been settled on the sofa, she didn't think she could face another upheaval while two men were delegated to cart her back up the stairs.

She felt as though she had been through a whole gamut of emotions that day, and acknowledged that a lot had happened. Not least that she had realised she had more of a passionate nature than she had thought. Oh, where had North Pole Northcott been when Sayre had kissed her?

And what about Sayre? She still hadn't fathomed out what he'd meant by that 'Think about it', though, truth to tell, she had a great deal of other things to think about.

She recalled how during dinner he hadn't given away that she'd been in a resigning or getting dismissed situation at Yarroll's, but had actually been there to help her—and she realised that while, of course, she didn't love him she did quite, well, like him.

She glanced his way—she had to look somewhere—and Maxine Hallam was still hanging on to his every word. Had *she* been invited this weekend for that special purpose? Oh, for goodness' sake! Astra felt annoyed with herself that it should bother her the tiniest scrap that Maxine and Sayre might be lovers.

It didn't bother her, not in the slightest, she was sure. But she was nevertheless very pleased when Greville came and stood close by her and blocked both Sayre and Maxine from her view.

'How are you feeling, sweetheart?' he wanted to know.

'Absolutely fine,' she assured him with a smile.

He looked sceptical, but smiled back just the same. 'You don't have to stand on ceremony if you'd prefer to go to bed and rest that foot,' he leaned down to quietly state.

'I don't want to cause a fuss,' she murmured.

'That settles it,' he decided, holding out his arms. 'What are big cousins for if not to carry little cousins when they're injured in battle?'

She laughed; she kind of adored him. But, before she could lever herself into a position where he could pick her up, Sayre had appeared from nowhere and it was his arms that were coming down for her, assuring Greville, 'The host's privilege, I think.'

Greville looked uncertain for a moment but gave way when Astra didn't make any protest—she was too stunned for that. And the next Astra knew was that Sayre had gathered her up in his arms and, amidst a general chorus of goodnights, plus Paul Caldwell complaining, 'I thought I'd got that privilege!' Sayre carried her from the room.

Why her heart should be racing so when she hadn't exerted herself in the smallest degree was a mystery to Astra. But she felt all racy and fluttery inside.

'Greville could have carried me,' she felt she should mention.

Sayre looked down at her. 'You object to my doing so?'

That would make it seem far more important than it was. Belatedly she found a strand of her cool image. 'Not at all,' she answered coolly. 'It's just that I feel a little guilty taking you away from Maxine...' damn, she hadn't meant to bring personal into this '... and your other guests.'

They rounded the stair head and Sayre started along the landing. At her bedroom door, he halted, then quietly, not making a big to-do about it, he said gallantly, 'Lovely though she is, Maxine and I are not an item.'

A smile began somewhere inside Astra. It took all the aloofness she could muster to hold it down. 'Never mind, Sayre,' she commented sweetly. 'You can't win them all,' said she who'd observed for herself that from what she'd seen Maxine had been giving him the green light every time she was near him. From what Astra had seen, Maxine would very much like it if she and Sayre were an item.

'I'll get you for that,' Sayre threatened, opening Astra's bedroom door and carrying her in.

A laugh escaped her. She didn't want it to, but it did. Sayre deposited her gently on her bed, her legs stretched out in front of her, and she knew that in a few more seconds he would be gone and she would be alone. Strangely, she didn't want him to go, not just yet.

'You never did say why you didn't go to the point-to-point today.' She delayed him, felt embarrassed, and added quickly, 'Not that you have any need to—say why you didn't go, I mean.' Oh, grief, this was terrible. 'Goodnight,' she said swiftly, and went a shade pink as Sayre looked sardonically down at her.

But, when she was dying a thousand deaths, 'You can't get rid of me that easily,' he drawled. 'As host I have to see you comfortably settled.'

'I am—comfortably settled. Goodn—'

'I decided against going when I judged it might be a good idea for Ellen to try the point-to-point without having me around.'

'It seems to have gone well,' Astra said thoughtfully.

'Ellen was with people who care for her,' he answered, and Astra knew he would never have let Ellen host the point-to-point group alone had that not been so. Did Sayre know, perhaps suspect, that Greville so cared for Ellen that he would protect her with his life if need be?

But that was Greville's secret, and, wanting to get away from the subject of caring in case she slipped up and gave away that Greville was in love with Ellen, Astra unthinkingly said that first other thing that came into her head—something she had puzzled and puzzled at.

'What did you mean, earlier…?' She broke off. Oh, good heavens above! She didn't want to go on. Oh, why had she got started? Hadn't she been striving all evening to forget about earlier?

'Earlier?' Sayre perched himself on the edge of the bed, seeming, despite a houseful of other guests, in no particular rush to get back to them.

'When—er—you said "Think about it" when…' She had no need to go on.

'You haven't worked it out?'

'I'm clever with figures.'

He grinned, and she found his grin most devastating. 'You've just not been educated in the right sphere,' he suggested. 'Though it shouldn't be so very difficult to work out.'

'Blame it on the wine. It must have dulled my brain,' she said lightly. And, really knowing she was going to feel embarrassed again any minute now—she should never have alluded to his 'Think about it'—'I wasn't going to mention it,' she began to apologise—only he cut in.

'You didn't drink more than half a glass.'

'With strong painkillers on board, I'd have been dancing a highland fling if I'd taken more.'

'Not with that foot.'

She stared at him. 'How did you know I had only half a glass?'

'Let's say I appreciate my guests having a good time.'

Ah! She had caught his eyes on her a time or two. As a good host he must obviously have glanced around the table many times during the evening, checking that no one was feeling left out.

'It was a good evening,' she said nicely.

'You seemed to be enjoying it.'

'Paul Caldwell's a very funny man.'

Sayre looked at her seriously. 'Smitten?' he asked, with not a smile about him.

'What sort of question's that to ask an out-of-work financial planner?' she asked, surprised. And, remembering, she added, 'Thank you, Sayre, for coming to my rescue—work-wise.'

He nodded. But repeated, 'Smitten?'

She laughed. 'Why, the dog with a bone!'

'It's of interest to me to know if it all started here.'

She wanted to smile again, but on thinking about it—she didn't. She didn't want a relationship with any man—Astra didn't have a smile in her. Her look became cool, frosty. 'Sorry to disappoint.' She clipped out the words. 'There'll be no wedding bells, if that answers your question.' Nor did she want marriage with any man.

Sayre's dark eyes assessed the cool, aloof look of her, and several seconds ticked by as he studied her remote expression. 'It does,' he replied, going on, 'Which leads me to answer yours.'

'Mine?' She gave him a chilly look. 'You mean *yours*. Your "Think about it" answer?'

He inclined his head in agreement, but, setting it out so that she would not have to puzzle again at his answer after he had gone, he explained, 'The reason why we stopped our delightful excursion on the perimeters of lovemaking...' He broke off. 'Did anybody ever tell you that you look even more fantastic when you blush?'

'Shut up,' she said, 'and for your information I never used to blush until I met you.' Then, wishing she hadn't told him that, she countermanded her previous order for him to shut up, and found, in spite of wishing that he would just clear off, that she was encouraging him. 'You were saying?'

He paused to give her a straight look, before he proceeded. 'So—it suddenly dawned on me—at a most inappropriate moment, I have to say—that making love to a virgin could have complications I'd prefer to avoid.'

Astra stared at him uncomprehendingly for a moment or two, and then went pink again when she thought she saw what he was getting at. 'I might get pregnant?' she questioned coolly, if a touch self-consciously.

'I was thinking more that you wouldn't know the rules.'

She had a feeling he was baiting her. 'Rules?' she enquired acidly.

'It came to me that, not knowing the rules, the way these things work, you might be the clinging type,' he corrected her.

'Clinging!' She was furious on the instant. 'From gratitude obviously,' she hurled at him sarcastically.

Her sarcasm glanced off him. She saw his lips twitch and felt her head-punching tendencies roar into life again, when pleasantly he enlightened her, 'You might want marriage.'

Marriage? Never! How dared he? 'To you?' She was almost bursting into flames in her fury. 'Don't flatter yourself, Baxendale. I...'

'You're too splendid for words when you're angry,' he observed, seeming to take pleasure in watching the twin patches of high colour in her cheeks.

Astra was about to go for his jugular, but just then caught

something, perhaps a glint of wickedness in his dark eyes, that stayed her. And she took a shaky but controlling breath. 'You did it on purpose!' she accused. He didn't ask what. 'You deliberately made me angry.'

'You've rumbled me,' he agreed, his mouth twitching.

'Why?' she questioned belligerently.

He considered her for a moment. 'You're terrific with your hair down,' he drawled.

Her hair was up. But Astra suddenly had the answer to why he had deliberately provoked her. Earlier that day, as he had reminded her, he had seen her with her hair down, had seen her a warm and, albeit inexperienced, a passionate woman. Quite clearly he preferred that image of her to the cool, arrogant female who faced him just now. Quite clearly he had thought to prod that passionate woman into angry life.

'Close the door on your way out!' she ordered imperiously.

She came the closest she had ever come to hitting him when, ignoring her imperious command, he asked nicely, 'You don't want me to stay and help you undress?'

The diabolical swine, he was still at it. Still trying to cut her down to size—even if she had started it by giving him the cool, frosty treatment. 'Good though I don't doubt you are in that area, I can manage quite well on my own,' she informed him woodenly—and nearly went into heart failure when he stood up, but only to come closer where he leaned down and appeared to be about to give her a kiss goodnight.

No! Everything in her shrieked, No! She couldn't allow him to kiss her. He had kissed her before and ever since then she had been in a state of anxiety. She was weak where he was concerned; she knew that now. She had to be on her guard against men like Sayre Baxendale.

His head came nearer. She panicked. She pushed him away hard. 'No!' she protested. 'Don't you do that!' she yelled, on the verge of hysteria in her fear of being loose-morecalled.

Her panic-stricken tone was not lost on Sayre, and he pulled back immediately. 'Hey. It's okay.' He attempted to calm her. 'There's no need to panic.' His tone was soothing and very different from the semi-baiting tone it had been earlier. 'I won't kiss you if you don't want me to.'

She stared at him, her eyes saucer-wide, the outer casing she had always protected herself with to others apart from family starting to fracture. 'I...' she tried helplessly, wanting her cool, aloof exterior back; she couldn't cope without it. She felt wide open, exposed—and vulnerable.

'What is it?' Sayre asked gently, close still, but not coming any nearer. 'What troubles you, Astra?' he pressed, his gentle tone doing absolutely nothing in the way of helping her get herself back together again. She shook her head speechlessly. Unhurriedly, taking care not to alarm her, he came and sat on the side of her bed again and reached for her hand. 'You're trembling,' he said, her shaking communicating itself to him. 'Is it me?' She had never seen him so serious. 'Oh, my...' He broke off. '*Is* it me? Do I frighten you? Oh, sweetheart, I wouldn't force myself on you,' he assured her softly, his tone so gentle, so tender, so understanding that she could have wept from the sensitivity of it.

'I know,' she choked huskily, finding her voice, wanting quite desperately to let him know that she wasn't afraid of him—she had an idea he'd be aghast should any woman be afraid of him. Look at the supportive way he looked after his sister. 'It isn't...' Her voice petered out. How could she tell him of her fears, her discovery that she might be like her mother and her two aunts after all?

Then she found that Sayre was quite capable of working some things out for himself, although thankfully he couldn't possibly know about her family history. His brow went back, and she knew for sure that something had just occurred to him when he murmured, 'Oh, Astra. It isn't me you're afraid of...' And, never more perceptive, he continued, 'It's yourself.'

Astra stared at him. She quite desperately wanted to tell him not to be absurd as she had earlier that day. But he wasn't being absurd—and she rather thought he knew it. 'Leave it,' she said, and had never felt quite so miserable as she did at that moment. All her defences seemed to have crumbled around her.

'Oh, my dear, how can I?' Sayre asked softly, far too perceptive, and apparently aware of her deep unhappiness.

'You've guests...'

'You're a guest—and since I had to come and deliver my invitation personally that makes you a very special guest,' he decreed, a teasing kind of note there.

His teasing worked. Astra smiled. Sayre moved to sit further on the bed, changing his position so that he could place an arm about her shoulders. It was a friendly arm, a coaxing arm, and Astra felt worried that she didn't feel threatened by it—that she felt comforted to have this man's arm about her.

'Want to tell me about it?'

Yesterday she would have angrily snapped 'What's to tell?'. Today, that evening, while she felt so down, so defeated, the anger and fight seemed to have drained from her. 'Nope,' she answered. 'And your other guests are waiting.'

She felt what might have been a kiss to the top of her head, and jerked to look at him. 'I suppose if I don't soon go your protective cousin Greville will...' Sayre broke off. 'Is that why he's so protective—because he knows how you've come to be so emotionally knotted up?'

Anger sparked into life—and Astra was glad of it. 'Leave

Greville out of this!' she snapped—and had to bear Sayre's questioning scrutiny.

'My, my, a mutual protection society,' he drawled.

And that did it. Angrily Astra pulled out of his arm. And Sayre let her go. But he was still close when, an abundance of charm suddenly there, 'Are you going to kiss me good-night?' he asked—much the same as he'd asked for a good-bye kiss at lunchtime.

'You do push your luck,' Astra replied haughtily.

His reply was to grin wickedly. 'Come on, Astra,' he pleaded. 'You wouldn't send me to bed worrying about you.'

Like *he'd worry* about her! Like *he* was going to *bed*! Where he was going was downstairs where, no matter what he'd said about him and Maxine Hallam not being an item, he would go back to sit near her and, without so much as a murmur, 'suffer' her pawing him.

'Want to bet?' Astra replied sharply.

But suddenly Sayre became serious. 'Do you need any help—with a zip or anything?' And Astra knew he was on the point of going back to his other guests. She shook her head. 'I can get Ellen to come up if you...' he began to offer.

'I can manage,' Astra cut in, liking him again, because clearly if the thought of him unzipping her upset her he would have no hesitation in calling his sister to assist her.

He smiled then and, at his most charming, enquired, 'I need to know you're not scared of me, green eyes. If I promise to be good, could I have that kiss?'

Her heart started to race idiotically. She wanted to kiss him. Just a light kiss. That wasn't being loose-moralled, was it? Some imp of wickedness suddenly awoke in her and she batted back at him the words he had used earlier that day. 'If you'd close your eyes for a second...'

Sayre stared at her, his look gentle. Then he closed his

eyes. Astra looked at him, looked at his handsome face and glanced down to his wonderful mouth—and felt an irresistible urge to kiss him. He had invited her to kiss him after all...

She leant forward and, very briefly, if a shade nervously, she touched her mouth to his. She pulled a little way back and Sayre opened his eyes. 'All right, sweetheart?' he asked softly.

She felt mesmerised by him. 'Fine,' she said chokily, and was unsure then if he moved forward first, or if she did. What she was sure about, as Sayre gently took her in his arms, was that—as he placed his mouth over hers while holding her tenderly, almost as if he feared she might break—never had she known such a beautiful kiss.

Then, unhurriedly, Sayre was pulling back. 'Get some rest,' he said softly, and took his arms from around her.

'I will,' she answered, her voice a whisper.

'Goodnight, sweet maid,' he smiled.

Astra couldn't afterwards remember if she had answered him. But later, after she had hobbled around getting ready for bed, she lay wide awake thinking of the two times Sayre Baxendale had embraced her that day.

One embrace had ended with them kissing passionately, Sayre making her emotions soar to undreamt of heights. The other had been so gentle, so giving, not taking, so beautiful. Was it any wonder she was wide awake?

CHAPTER SIX

ASTRA slept only fitfully. She had not expected to sleep well, and didn't. The fact that her injured ankle was troublesome was the least of it. If she moved, the pain woke her up. If she woke up, she thought of Sayre. If she thought of Sayre, she thought of her responses to him. But she didn't want to think of her responses to him. By far would she prefer to be North Pole Northcott!

She was glad when daylight arrived. Not many hours from now the household would start to stir, then Greville would come and help her downstairs and would drive her home. While Astra still thought Abberley a lovely house, she would take jolly good care not to accept another invitation here. Not that Sayre would ever invite her again. Sayre...

She tried to get some more sleep but was wide awake and contemplating hobbling to take a bath when, a few minutes before seven, the door to her room was quietly opened and there stood the man she had spent a good deal of time trying to eject from her thoughts.

Sayre came in, quietly closing the door. 'Thank you for knocking,' Astra said acidly—it was that or smile at the wretched man.

'I didn't want to disturb you if you were asleep,' he replied, coming over to the bed and standing looking down at her. 'What sort of a night did you have?' he enquired, dragging his gaze back from her cloud of red hair.

No make-up on, her hair loose and no doubt looking a mess, Astra no longer felt like smiling. What she felt was a wreck. 'Quite good,' she lied primly.

He didn't look convinced, but let it go. 'How's the ankle?'

'I've decided not to go on the march today.'

'So let me have a look.'

Cheek! Who did he think he was—her physician? No way. 'It's fine.'

'Still swollen?' he enquired, and, clearly having read from her obstinate look that he didn't stand a dog's chance of checking her ankle for himself, to her amazement he did no less than whip back the duvet.

Astra was furious—and scarlet. If it wasn't enough to have to sit there with her hair all tousled, all sign of sophistication very far away, it was just not to be borne to have to sit there with her silk and lace wisp of a nightdress ridden halfway up her thighs. 'Do you very much mind?' she snapped, beginning to think her complexion would be permanently scarlet if she had much more of him.

She tried to pull the duvet back—he wasn't having it. The bandage had come off in the night and he had gently taken a hold of her foot. But even while he wasn't looking at her but was addressing his remarks to the foot he was examining he was making her aware that nothing of her appearance had passed him by.

'That's a very fetching garment you're nearly wearing,' he remarked to her swollen ankle.

Oh, if only he was nearer, just six inches nearer would be enough for her to clout his ear. 'Nobody packs their old clothes when they go away for the weekend,' she retorted icily as, his inspection over, he replaced the duvet and came to perch himself close up to her on the edge of the bed.

'Oh, Astra,' he said softly. 'Put your defences away. I know, better than anyone, that you aren't wearing it for my benefit.'

'For your benefit I wouldn't be wearing it at all!' she snapped smartly.

He laughed. And, against what she very much knew that she should do, Astra found that she was laughing too. Sayre stared at her. 'You know, you're very lovely,' he said softly and, just as if he couldn't resist, he leaned forward and gently kissed her.

That set her off going all haywire again. She pulled back. 'Don't…'

'I won't,' he smiled, pulling back. 'That took me rather by surprise.' She stared at him——he hadn't intended to kiss her, it had just seemed to happen? 'It was nice, though,' he grinned.

She gave him a disgusted look, but inside her heart was laughing. 'I was just thinking of going to take a bath,' she said apropos of nothing, and was immediately cross with herself——why did she frequently feel embarrassed and idiotic when she was talking to him? 'I never used to be so gauche,' she told him belligerently.

He looked amused. 'You're going to lay that at my door as well as the blushing?'

'Who else's?' Astra got herself together. 'Thank you for calling,' she said, to let him know his visit was over.

He stayed where he was——plainly, nobody ever bossed Sayre Baxendale around. 'I'll get Ritchie Saunders to come and take a look at your ankle.'

'That won't be necessary,' she answered nicely. 'I'll get dressed as soon as I've had my bath, and Greville will drive me home.'

'Your cousin's not going back until this afternoon,' Sayre informed her lightly.

Astra drew a startled breath. She wanted to be away from Abberley with all speed——and yet part of her, a part she just didn't understand, felt a sudden uplifting of spirits to know she would be spending a few more hours here than she had thought. 'I——didn't know that.' She had been sure

Greville had said they would be leaving on Sunday morning. 'Greville...' she began.

'Greville doesn't know himself yet,' Sayre cut in solemnly.

Solemnly, too, was how Astra stared at him. All too obviously Sayre intended suggesting to her cousin that he delay his departure until after lunch. She knew in advance what Greville's answer would be. He was so in love with Ellen it would be hard enough for him to tear himself away from her as it was. He would just leap at the chance to spend more time in her company. Sayre had seen that, and must approve!

'I see,' Astra answered belatedly, by no chance ready to confirm his suspicions about Greville's feelings for his sister. 'Well, I'll still go and have my bath.'

'You don't think you should try and catch up on the sleep you missed until the good doctor's been?'

'Grateful though I am to the good doctor, I don't need him,' Astra replied pleasantly.

'Were you always this stubborn?'

She looked at him and smiled. 'Always,' she answered.

Sayre stood up. 'You don't need help getting in and out of the bath?'

'I'll call you if I do,' she lied prettily.

He looked amused. 'I've an idea you could end up being one of my favourite people,' he commented softly.

'Steady, Sayre. That's enough to send a rush of blood to any girl's head!' She heard him laugh on his way out. It was a very pleasing sound.

From spending a night that had crept along with torturous slowness, the next few hours seemed to positively speed by. The reason for that, however, was that she had a constant stream of visitors. Astra was still in her robe after her bath when Dr Richard Saunders paid her a visit.

'What size is the foot this morning?' he enquired pleasantly.

'The swelling's down, I'm sure,' Astra replied as he surveyed her ankle and strapped it up again.

'There's nothing broken, but try to keep off it as much as possible,' he advised.

No sooner had he gone than one of the housekeeper's helpers came with a tray of breakfast. But before Astra had downed more than a sip or two of orange juice Greville was there.

'Carry on eating, I've just had mine,' he smiled, giving her cheek a peck. 'How are you feeling?' he wanted to know.

'Fine,' she answered. 'How about you?'

'Never better,' he replied enthusiastically, and from the look on his face Astra just knew he was thinking of Ellen.

'Sayre's been in to see me.'

'I know, I've just seen Ellen.'

'Does she know we're invited to lunch?'

Greville smiled, his smile becoming a beam, a grin. 'Ellen thinks it would be a much better idea if you stayed on here, at Abberley, for a while,' he answered, and as Astra stared at him, the words 'No, no way' rushing to her lips, he was adding, 'And so do I.'

'You do? No!' She quickly squashed that very idea. 'No, I couldn't possibly stay.' The very idea was unthinkable.

'Oh, sweetheart. Why?' And before she could begin to tell him—good heavens, she had only come for his sake, anyway, and since he was leaving, albeit his departure was now put back until after lunch, there was no way he was leaving without her—her cousin was going on, 'It would help me tremendously if you'd agree to stay.'

'How?' she asked, even while she didn't want to know the answer. There was absolutely no question of her staying on so much as a minute after Greville had gone.

'Don't you see?' He didn't need any coaxing to swiftly tell her, 'With you here I have a ready made excuse to come down to Abberley every day to see for myself how you are.'

Oh, don't do this to me, Greville! 'I can't, Greville! It wouldn't be right. Yes, yes, I know it would be a chance for you to see more of Ellen, but you've got on so well with her this weekend surely...' Her voice faded when someone knocked at her door, and Paul Caldwell poked his head round.

'I'm just off. I couldn't go without popping up to say cheerio,' he said, coming further into the room, his admiring glance on her mane of red hair which she hadn't had a chance yet to do more than drag a brush through.

'I'll see you later,' Greville said to Astra, waiting a second or two to pick up if Astra, still not properly dressed, had any objection to being left alone in her bedroom with Paul.

Astra had too much else on her mind to worry about any such small matter. 'See you later,' she agreed. For goodness' sake—surely Greville couldn't be serious?

'Are you going to be very kind to me and let me have your phone number?' Paul Caldwell asked the moment the door had closed behind Greville.

'Er—I'm not sure where I'll be,' Astra prevaricated. Certainly not here! 'I'm thinking of going to stay with my aunt for a little while,' she invented. He didn't look as if he believed her. 'Until my ankle gets better,' she added to her sins.

'Let me know where your aunt lives; I'll call and bring you some flowers, some grapes.'

Astra laughed, she liked him. She did something she never did—she gave him her phone number—and he went off cheerfully, leaving her wondering once again about herself. It was odd but, having given him her phone number

and thereby permission to contact her, she didn't feel in
any way that the Jolliffe gene was at work. She didn't feel
wayward, or man-mad, or, to be precise, even interested in
Paul Caldwell at that level. What she felt, she realised—
the revelations about herself since Sayre had kissed her still
a cause of great concern—was friendly to Paul. If he
wanted to be friends then she felt she would be happy to
be just that with him. If Paul wanted more, then he should
save himself a phone call.

She was glad to have a few more visitors as Kit and
Vanessa Lister came to say goodbye and wish her a speedy
recovery. While she had someone with her it saved her
from the guilt she knew she would feel the moment she
was on her own.

And, true enough, the moment she had said goodbye to
the Listers, guilt rushed in. Greville had always been there
for her. He had been so hurt in the past. He was so happy
now. Agreed, anxious about his chances with Ellen, but
happy, so happy to be with Ellen. Oh, abomination—and
didn't she owe Greville. But rule out owing. She loved him
and there was no price on love.

Astra, her hair neatly in its usual knot, was still awash
with guilt over Greville, panicking that he must see that
she couldn't stay, when Ellen, bearing a walking stick and
an over-large slipper, came to see her. She apologised for
having not come sooner, explaining she had been seeing
everyone off. Ellen pulled up a bedroom chair close to the
one Astra was sitting in—and then voiced the question
Astra had been hoping not to hear.

'You will stay on with us, Astra, won't you?' Ellen asked
with a sweet smile.

'I…' Oh, crumbs, Astra found Ellen so difficult to say
no to. 'I can't,' she answered.

'Any particular reason?' Oh, heck, Ellen didn't look to

be so easily put off. 'You won't be going anywhere else with that foot, I'd say.'

Well, that was true enough. Astra wanted to say, as she had to Paul Caldwell, that she was going to stay with her aunt for a few days, but discovered she didn't want to lie to Ellen.

'It—wouldn't be fair to your brother,' Astra explained at last.

'Fair?' Ellen echoed. 'Oh, Astra, I promise you, Sayre...'

Astra shook her head. 'It wouldn't be right. Sayre only expected his home to be invaded for the weekend. And,' she added hurriedly, 'while you've both made us all more than welcome, and we've had a super time, I—don't feel it would be right,' she ended lamely, and refused to be persuaded otherwise.

Guilt was her companion again when Ellen had gone, and Astra limped to the wide window seat. She took her ease, realising she must look quite a sketch; she was wearing a classic summer dress that she was most thankful she had thought to pop into her case—what with her swollen ankle and the strapping her trousers would be too snug a fit to wear—and one flat walking shoe and one over-large slipper.

She took the slipper off and looked out of the window. It was so peaceful here. The treacherous thought came from out of nowhere that how pleasant it would be to linger on here for a while... Then, shaken that she should nurse such thoughts, Astra banished the traitorous notions.

She couldn't stay! How could she? Sayre didn't want her there as some extended weekend visitor. Oh, he would go along with it. Astra knew that if it would please his sister, during this time of help after her breakdown, then Sayre would not have a word to say against Ellen inviting any one of his guests to stay on. But Astra was sure he wouldn't want her there. What he would want was his home back to himself again.

Astra sighed and supposed she should think in terms of getting herself downstairs. She was about to move from her window seat when just then a couple rounded the side of the house and seemed to be setting off in the same direction she had taken yesterday for her walk. It was her cousin Greville and Ellen Morton. They were walking close together and appeared from that distance to be the best of companions.

Guilt was *Astra's* companion and she was torn all ways as, walking, talking, happy together, she watched the pair disappear from view. She couldn't stay—yet Greville deserved every scrap of happiness he could find. Would it be so wrong? It was lovely here. But Sayre didn't want her around, and that settled the issue.

She changed her mind about going downstairs and, in order to save time later, and with the aid of the walking stick, limped around her room putting her belongings together. She had her case on the bed and just had last night's dress to pack when the door behind her opened.

Astra turned as Sayre came and joined her by the bed, his eyes on her neatly folded garments as he remarked, 'I take it you don't go for my idea of staying and being cosseted by Ellen and Mrs Turner for a week or so?'

A week or so! Astra stared at him. '*Your* idea?' she questioned.

'You sound doubtful,' he observed. 'Here,' he offered, swinging a chair near. 'Take the weight off.'

'You really do think I'm fat?'

'Slender as a reed,' he bounced back at her. 'I just like to get you going.'

'Because you think I'm prim and proper. Not to mention haughty beyond the point of arrogance.'

'Stung, did it?'

'Shut up.'

'Is that any way to talk to your host for the next two weeks?'

Two weeks! 'You don't want me here,' she stated, taking the seat he'd turned round for her while he came and sat on the end of her bed.

His look was serious as he confessed, 'I realised after I left you this morning that it was true, as I mentioned before, I wasn't too happy at the thought of you going back to your home with no one there to look after you.'

Astra gazed at him in astonishment. 'You're going soft, Baxendale,' she jibed, getting herself together. And she was not at all sure how she felt about him not being too happy that she had no one to look after her. 'I'm not your responsibility,' she told him forthrightly.

'You injured yourself on my property,' he reminded her. But before she could give him some sharp answer to that he smiled his devastating smile, which stopped her dead in her tracks. 'Besides which,' he went on, 'your charms are getting to me, sweet Astra.' Her heart did a crazy kind of flip and, as her insides joined in the craziness, she looked away from him. 'I've embarrassed you again,' he said.

She looked at him in some exasperation. 'What *is* it about you?' she demanded. She knew he could cause her to feel embarrassed, but didn't take it kindly that *he* knew it too.

'My charm?' he suggested, and grinned. 'Come on, Astra, give in,' he coaxed.

She didn't want to give in. No way did she want to give in. 'Thank you,' she answered, and didn't know who was in charge of her when she added, 'I'd love to stay.' She didn't even object when he got up from the bed, squeezed her shoulder, and, as natural as you please, bent down and lightly kissed her.

She unpacked her belongings after he'd gone, wondering

if there was something in the air in this part of Buckinghamshire that caused her to think and feel, not to mention behave, so very differently from what she had believed she did normally.

He had kissed her and, when she didn't welcome any man's advances, she had enjoyed it. Correction—kisses. She wanted, and tried hard, to stay aloof from him, and yet found he could make her laugh in spite of herself. And what about just now when she had been positive that she had been going to stay at Abberley no longer than today—what had she done but folded completely and, against all logic, agreed to stay? It was all, she concluded, a total mystery to her.

Over the next few days she grew to know and like Ellen more and more. They went for drives, or chatted, or read and generally relaxed, and Astra discovered that Ellen was very good company.

Greville had arrived on Monday evening with the clothes Astra had asked him to collect. 'I'd ask Yancie or Fennia,' she had begun to explain, handing over the apartment key, 'but...'

'Oh, you can't do that.' Greville had seen the way her mind worked. 'They'd be down here like a shot if they knew you'd been injured. They'd both want to take you back with them. And that,' he ended succinctly, 'would ruin everything.'

Astra had laughed. While her thoughts had been more in the direction of not imposing herself on her two cousins in this lovely honeymoon period for them both, Greville—while he might have thought similarly—was more concerned that he had an excuse to come to Abberley.

Greville had stayed to dinner on Monday evening, and on Tuesday he arrived just after dinner with something he had 'forgotten' to bring for Astra the previous evening.

'Why not join us for a meal tomorrow?' Sayre suggested, when Greville made noises about leaving.

'Actually, I was wondering if I might make it a table for four somewhere locally,' Greville answered pleasantly. 'Astra's getting about much more easily now than she was a couple of days ago, and I'd like to repay a little of your generous hospitality.'

Sayre flicked a glance to Astra and then to his sister, and graciously accepted for them. 'I think I'll go up to my room,' Astra decided once Greville had gone, and bade Ellen and her brother goodnight, only to find Sayre strolling to the staircase with her.

'Your cousin's right—you are walking better than you were,' Sayre observed, suiting his steps to hers.

'It's all this rest,' Astra answered. 'I can't remember a time when I was so lazy.'

'Enforced laziness,' Sayre documented for her as they halted at the bottom of the stairs. But, giving her a direct look, he enquired, 'Still hate me for my part in causing you to resign?'

Astra looked up at him. 'From my point of view it could have been handled better,' she answered honestly. 'That is, if my client had contacted me personally and asked me to check, I'd have done so just as thoroughly. Though the outcome would have been just the same,' she admitted. 'I'd have still resigned.'

Sayre looked steadily at her for long, long moments. Then he asked, 'Know something, Astra Northcott?' She looked at him and waited. 'Any time you're ready to take up your career again, I'd be glad to have you on my staff.'

Astra stared at him, quite speechless for some seconds. Then, 'Wow!' she gasped. 'When you apologise for your original opinion of me, you really apologise.'

Sayre looked down at her, saw the mischief in her eyes. 'You knew I'd changed my opinion—though I'm beginning to think there's even far more to you than I first realised,' he said slowly.

At which she froze. In her view he already knew a very great deal more about her than any man had a right to know. 'Goodnight, Sayre,' she bade him shortly.

He looked down into her unsmiling eyes. 'I suppose a goodnight kiss is out of the question?' he had the diabolical nerve to ask.

A hot retort sprang to her lips, but, remembering his penchant for trying to cut her down to size whenever she became in the slightest haughty, she swallowed the words down. She smiled, a pretty smile. 'I wonder, how does one tell one's host to get lost, without appearing rude?' she enquired pleasantly.

She could have hit him that he laughed. And wanted to hit him even harder as hearing him laugh made her want to laugh, to join in. She wouldn't, of course. But then, suddenly, neither of them was laughing because all at once, as Sayre looked down at her, there was a tension in the air.

They stared at each other and her throat went dry. His head started to come nearer. She wanted to say 'Don't' but she couldn't speak. Then Sayre's arms were reaching for her, and he was holding her, and when what she was sure she wanted to do was to push him away somebody else seemed to take charge of her, and she took a step forward.

Their lips met and Sayre held her close up against him. His arms tightened about her and it felt so good. Then he broke his kiss and stared down at her. She stared back, everything all at once haywire. He smiled encouragingly and she found a small smile, and his head came down again, and once more he kissed her.

Her heart was racing—suddenly Astra was starting to panic! He had kissed her before, seriously kissed her, and she'd had to live through a nightmare of anxiety about herself and her fear of that family gene ever since.

She drew back with a gasp. 'I th-think...' she said shakily. Coughed, and started again. 'I think that's enough of that,' she stated primly.

Sayre took a step back as if he wasn't quite believing this—or her. His mouth twitched, just as if he found her old-fashioned in the extreme. 'And quite right too,' he agreed. His arms dropping to his sides, he took another step back and, just as if she were some ancient maiden aunt, 'Do you need any help with the stairs?' he enquired nicely.

Astra gave him a haughty, aloof look—and this time he let her get away with it. She went to bed knowing that, Greville or no Greville, she was going home in the morning.

By morning, however, the incident seemed less magnified than it had the previous evening. Anyhow, Greville would spend all that day looking forward to seeing Ellen that night. How could she ring him up from her apartment and tell him she was home?

Astra was still at Abberley that afternoon when the telephone rang. Ellen was outside chatting to the gardener and Astra hesitated; by the time she had limped as fast as she could to get Ellen, the caller might have rung off.

With no one else answering it, Astra picked up the phone, and was straight away recalling being held firmly in Sayre's arms last night. 'How's the delightful redhead this afternoon?' he asked.

She felt warm colour surge to her cheeks and was momentarily stumped—she just wasn't used to replying in any way but coolly to such comments. Yet she was this man's guest, and she knew, to her cost, that any hint of haughtiness on her part would see Sayre bettering her.

'I'm sure you must be busy,' was the best she could come up with as a non-cool reply. Sayre had been in her mind a great deal—it worried her.

'I am actually,' he answered her. 'Which is why I rang.'

'I'll get Ellen. She's...'

'You'll do no such thing.'

'But...'

'Sweet Astra—you don't need the exercise.'

'So go on—charm me!' He laughed, and Astra felt a warm glow inside. But that would never do. 'So you're busy, and...'

'And I'm going to be too late to join the three of you tonight.'

Why did she feel so disappointed? Nonsense! Of course it wasn't disappointment. 'Do you want me to ask Mrs Turner to leave you a meal or...?'

'I'll get something sent in. If you'd just tell Ellen I can't make it.'

'Right. Goodb—'

'And Astra.'

'Yes.'

'Enjoy your evening.'

'Goodbye,' she said, and put down the phone to discover that her hand was actually shaking. Lecture time coming up.

Astra went to her room and tried to push her anxieties away. Come on, get yourself together, do. Just because Baxendale has charm by the bucketful and he kissed you, and you liked it—it isn't a catastrophe. You aren't promiscuous. If you were, you'd have been all over Paul Caldwell when he was here. As for Baxendale causing you to feel all shaky inside, well, grief, you're not used to—well—um—men like him.

Feeling impatient with herself, with her thoughts, with those years of fearing, as might still be the case, that she had more of her mother's family's genes in her than her father's, Astra was about to go downstairs again to tell Ellen about her brother's phone call, when she checked.

Just a minute. Did she want to play gooseberry to Ellen

and Greville? She certainly did not. Furthermore, Astra suddenly realised that if she could find some excuse not to go out to dinner with them, then Greville would have Ellen all to himself. Greville would be highly pleased at the chance.

Sayre might be cross, of course... Oh, for heaven's sake, why did she have to keep thinking of him all the time? Anyway, how could he be cross? Didn't she know her cousin for the darling he was? Didn't she know of his love for Ellen? Just as Astra knew how much Sayre watched over his sister, so she knew without one doubt that never, ever would Greville do anything to hurt Ellen.

Astra delayed going down to Ellen when something else occurred to her. If she told Ellen now that she wouldn't be going with them, Ellen might well say that she wasn't going either. Ellen might well suggest she telephone her cousin to call off the dinner arrangements. Oh, that would never do.

Astra knew then that she was going to delay telling Ellen about her 'headache' until after Greville was on his way. Much better, Astra decided; headaches were known to clear up in an hour. She'd better have hers just before Greville was due to arrive.

In fact Astra stayed in her room so long it was Ellen who came to seek her out. She found Astra lying on top of her bed. 'Oh, good,' she smiled in her sweet way. 'I was hoping you were resting that ankle—that's why I didn't come earlier.'

Astra glanced at her foot and, knowing she was a hopeless liar, kept her eyes down. 'I've a bit of a headache, actually,' she said, and, instantly feeling a fraud—*The things I do for you, Greville Alford*—added, 'I'm sure it will soon be better.'

'Have you taken anything for it?' Ellen was instantly sympathetic.

'I'm up to my ears in painkillers,' Astra smiled.

Straightaway Ellen said she would leave her to rest, and that perhaps Astra would manage to have a pain-relieving nap before they went out.

Astra started to have second thoughts about what she was doing when Ellen left her. Then she remembered Greville's goodness to her over the years, and reminded herself it was only dinner, for heaven's sake. Just a few private hours where Greville and Ellen might get to know a little more about each other with no one else around. Greville was totally in love with Ellen, and it wasn't as if Ellen didn't like Greville. Hadn't she seen for herself the way she laughed in his company?

There was half an hour to go before her cousin was due to arrive when Astra got off her bed and went along to Ellen's room. Ellen, in a house coat, was seated before her dressing-table mirror applying lipstick.

Astra saw her glance to the same clothes she had been wearing earlier, and quickly asked, 'Would you mind very much if I didn't come with you this evening, Ellen?'

'Oh, your poor head.' Ellen was more worried about her than that she wouldn't be joining them, and Astra felt dreadful—and made herself remember why she was doing this.

'I'm sorry,' she apologised, trying to keep her perjury down to a minimum. Feeling a touch breathless as she geared herself up for the big one: 'I did tell you that Sayre rang, didn't I?'

'Sayre rang?'

'I didn't? I'm sorry, my head must be more muddled than I thought! Um—he's working late.'

'He can't make dinner?' Ellen realised, and as the implication of both of them not being at dinner dawned Astra was positive she saw a trace of a fleeting smile light Ellen's eyes and mouth before—perhaps over the years she'd become used to masking her emotions—she hid what she was inwardly feeling.

'Sayre said he'd get something sent in,' Astra informed her, and, feeling swamped by guilt, added, 'I think I'll go back to bed,' and discovered Ellen was quite as lovely and unselfish as Greville thought.

'Your dinner! I've given Mrs Turner the night off, but it won't take but a minute to whip you up an omelette.'

'I couldn't eat a thing,' Astra invented, having not given a thought to her own dinner, but accepting she was going to have to pay for her sins by going to bed supperless. 'I'll leave you to get ready,' she said, wished Ellen a lovely evening, and limped back to her room.

She later heard Greville arrive, but wasn't up to lying to him as, in front of Ellen, she would have to, so stayed in her room. Twenty minutes later there was a tap on her door and Greville came in carrying a tray.

He gave her a sympathetic kiss once he had set the omelette and bacon down on the side table. 'How's the head? I didn't know you suffered from headaches.'

'You shouldn't have!' she exclaimed, indicating the tray. 'And...' since she didn't need to lie to him '...in the cause of true love—I don't.'

'You...' He stared at her. Then he smiled the most beautiful smile. 'You're wonderful!' he laughed. Quite obviously he knew Sayre was working late and considered it no hardship to dine à deux with Ellen.

'Invite me to the wedding,' she answered.

'Come the day,' he hoped, high on happiness at the thought of the evening before him. 'Thanks, kiddo,' he said, and kissed her cheek again, but, as if not wanting to miss another second of Ellen's company, left in a hurry.

Astra had her meal and made her slow way down to the kitchen where she washed and dried her used dishes and suddenly realised, quite panic-stricken, exactly what she

had done. It was all very well thinking herself exceedingly
clever that she had got Greville and Ellen dining as a twosome, but where did that leave Astra Northcott? A twosome
with Sayre when he came home, that was where.

She had no idea, of course, at what time Sayre might
come home. But she was not waiting around downstairs to
find out. Going as fast as she could given that her ankle,
though much improved, was still proving bothersome, Astra
returned to her room, and only felt safe once she'd arrived
there.

Safe! There was that word again. Good grief, anybody
would think she felt threatened by Sayre. Nonsense!

When darkness had descended and he wasn't home,
Astra decided she might as well go to bed. She showered,
cleaned her teeth, donned one of the fresh nightdresses
Greville had brought, brushed out her hair and got into bed.
She took up her paperback.

Sayre... She pushed him out of her head. Read five lines,
and he was back there again. Oh, confound it! What was
it? What plagued her about him? Before she could find an
answer she heard a car coming up the drive. Her heart
suddenly started to misbehave. It was late, but unless they'd
gobbled their food it was too early for it to be Greville and
Ellen returning.

Astra heard Sayre come in and strained her ears, listening
for what he might be doing. The downstairs room would
have been in darkness. Perhaps he'd gone to the kitchen to
make himself some coffee, perhaps a snack. Oh. Her straining ears heard a sound like someone coming up the stairs.
Sayre had to pass her room to get to his. She heard him
coming along the landing. She knew he would go by without looking in.

She was mistaken. Her door opened and, there, tall,
good-looking, holding his jacket over his shoulder by one
finger, was Sayre. He looked tired and, remembering the

pressure she had sometimes been under on her busier than usual office days, Astra immediately felt for him.

But speechlessly she stared at him. 'Well, well,' he drawled—just that, and she wanted to laugh. What was it about him? He came over to her and she put down her book and drew the duvet up to her chin. 'There was I certain you'd gone out leaving your light on so I shouldn't feel lonely—and what do I find?'

Astra wanted to smile, but looked away. 'I had a headache,' she lied, and went a bit pink because of her lie.

Sayre sat on the edge of her bed and, it seemed, had seen her lie for what it was.

'A convenient headache?' he enquired.

Her eyes went to his. 'You're not annoyed?' she asked, rushing on, 'Greville will take good care of Ellen; I know he will.'

'If he gives her half the care I've seen him give you, I'm sure I'll have no need to be annoyed,' Sayre replied blandly.

'Greville...'

'Has always taken care of you?'

'I wasn't going to say that!' What she had been going to say was that her cousin was good and kind, to try to impress on Sayre the terrific qualities Greville possessed. But she supposed that Sayre had sorted out for himself that he needn't worry about the man his emotionally battered sister was out with, because otherwise he would be back out again racing to collect Ellen.

'But he has?'

'Taken care of me?' Sayre didn't answer, and, recalling Greville's part in her life, 'I was more fortunate than Yancie and Fennia—I still had my father,' Astra explained.

And realised it explained nothing when Sayre enquired, 'How did Yancie and Fennia get into this? Who, indeed, are Yancie and Fennia?'

Astra laughed and then shook her head. It seemed incredible to her—when a week ago she would have been scandalised at the notion—that she should be sitting in bed dressed only in her nightdress chatting away to some man and feeling so comfortable about it, she had actually laughed. That thought suddenly brought an icy chill to her spine, and, horror-struck, she stared at him.

'What is it?' Sayre asked urgently, the change in her from laughing-eyed to horror-struck so startling, he moved closer, bending nearer as if to help.

'N-nothing,' she said hoarsely. 'Would you go, please?'

'Not a chance!' he answered, no two ways about it. 'You're terrified of something. I…'

'I'm all right!' She chopped him off shortly, giving him an exasperated look. He ignored it.

'So what's wrong with Yancie and Fennia that terrifies you so?'

Astra tried to get herself back together again. 'N-nothing,' she repeated, and added, since it didn't look as though he'd go until she told him *something*, 'Yancie and Fennia are my cousins. The three of us were more or less brought up together. We're close.' Her voice was coming out staccato fashion. She didn't seem able to control it. 'Our mothers are sisters. We were at boarding-school together—from the age of seven…' She broke off. 'I'm gabbling.'

'No, you're not,' he contradicted. 'Go on,' he insisted.

'What do you mean, "Go on"?' Astra challenged snappily, starting to feel aggrieved. 'There's nothing to *go on* with.' She was trembling, she knew she was; why didn't he just clear off so she could get herself back together?

'What happened to your cousins?' Sayre tried another tack to try and prise from her what had caused her to be so horrified a minute ago.

'Nothing has happened to them! Will you go?' she demanded. He said nothing, and didn't move but just sat steadily eyeing her. 'They got married—that's what happened!' Astra blurted out in a rush.

'Unhappily married?' Sayre asked evenly, as if that might be where the answer lay. 'Is that…?'

'They are both extremely happily married!' Astra flew defensively. 'The last time I saw them, only a couple of weeks ago as a matter of fact, they were both quite blissfully happily married!'

'But you're not blissful that they should be so happy?' Sayre probed. Astra was outraged at the very suggestion.

'Nothing could be further from the truth!' she flared—and went unwarily charging straight into his trap. 'We worried for so long, the three of us. But they knew, they found out—and it must be the most wonderful feeling of release in the world—that they haven't inherited…' She stopped, aghast, as she suddenly realised what in her fire-and-brimstone outrage she was saying.

But Sayre, to her annoyance, did not seem prepared to let her leave it there. 'Haven't inherited what?' he asked, his look steady on her, his tone calm and seeming every bit as if he was prepared to wait all night for an answer if need be.

'Inherited nothing,' she flew belligerently.

He wasn't having that. 'Come on, Astra,' he coaxed. And when she stared stubbornly at him and refused to say another word he said, 'You've said so much—tell me more about this most wonderful feeling of release in the…'

'I wouldn't know about it!' she cut him off huffily.

'But your two cousins do. What was it that they found out—that released them from the worry the three of you had lived with for so long?'

'It's none of your business!' Astra tossed at him angrily, hoping to offend him. That might make him clear off and leave her alone.

Water off a duck's back! 'I'm making it my business,' he answered, not in the least offended.

'Tough!' she jibed.

Much good did it do her. She had noted his dog-with-a-bone tendency before. That tendency was out in full force when he stayed on the trail.

'It has something to do with why you're so repressed, why...'

'I'm *not* repressed!' she yelled. Honestly! This man!

'Why you're so afraid of your emotional responses,' he went on just as if she hadn't so fiercely interrupted. 'This is the crux of why you're so frozen up inside. So inhibited...'

Frozen up! Inhibited! 'I've had just about enough of you, Baxendale!' she raged.

He smiled pleasantly—she read her own word 'tough' in his smile. 'What was it that your two cousins found out, but you didn't?' he asked, he as stubborn as she—Astra, to her fury, was just discovering.

'Oh, why don't you just clear off?' she raged angrily.

'Tell me and I will. Tell me what it is you fear you've inherited.'

He was sharp, much too sharp, much too clever at reading that which was only sketchily hinted at.

'Goodnight!' Astra bade him firmly, and lay down in her bed and closed her eyes. If he was so sharp he wouldn't need a bigger hint than that that he was wasting his time.

She heard him give an exaggerated sigh, and wanted to open her eyes, but wouldn't. Open them she did, though, and was furiously angry straight away when she distinctly heard him say, 'Sleep tight, Astra.' A pause, then he said, 'I'm sure you won't mind if I ask your cousin Greville what...'

Her eyes flew wide and she struggled to sit up. 'Don't you *dare*!' she snapped. He smiled, and she didn't just want to hit him, she wanted to kill him. 'Greville doesn't know... That is, he knows the family background. Of course he knows that!' Astra hurled at Sayre, and then found she was rushing on into speech like somebody wound up, like somebody with a long held spring just freed—and she couldn't stop, no matter how much she wanted to. Angrily she faced Sayre Baxendale to fling at him, 'Greville knows about my mother, Yancie's mother and Fennia's mother—the three Jolliffe women are half sisters to Greville's mother, if you must know. But, while Greville knows—of course he does—about his aunts' fast and loose ways...' She broke off—she hadn't meant to say that. 'You're confusing me!' Astra accused on a shaky breath, and saw the quick intelligence in Sayre's eyes as he took in what she had said so far and quickly sifted through it.

She felt him take a gentle hold of her hand, and had no idea when she had put it outside the duvet. 'Am I right in thinking that this thing you think you've inherited—you and your cousins—is something to do with the fast and loose ways of your mothers?' Sayre asked gently—and Astra's fierce fury all at once evaporated.

'Oh, don't tell Greville—or talk about it with him,' she pleaded. 'He knows all about the way his aunts carry on, of course,' she explained. 'But, while he's been an absolute love to me, Fennia and Yancie, he's had such a tough time himself, emotionally—I don't want him to now start worrying that, with Fennia and Yancie released, I'm left with this terrible fear.'

Sayre was still holding her hand. 'What terrible fear would that be, my dear?' he asked softly.

Astra stared at him in amazement. He was quick, he was clever, he... 'You must have...' she gasped. 'Promiscuity,' she said. 'The Jolliffe gene. Yancie, Fennia and me—we worried for years that...'

The utter astonishment on Sayre's face caused her to break off. 'You think you may be promiscuous!' Sayre cut in, and actually seemed as if he might burst out laughing at the very thought. He didn't laugh, however, but, astonishment still showing, his intelligence having been at work, he probed gently, 'You think—fear—you may have inherited some fast and loose gene from your mother?' He stared at her, dumbfounded. 'Oh, Astra, Astra, Astra,' he said softly. 'Come here and let Uncle Sayre tell you a few facts of life.' With that, Astra was suddenly feeling too shaken by all that had taken place to resist, Sayre gathered her into his arms, tucking her head into his shoulder.

It was like coming home after being out in some tumultuous storm, in the safe harbour of Sayre's arms. But fears grown over so many years were not so easily vanquished. 'Sayre, I…'

'Shh,' he breathed to the top of her head. 'Listen, and trust me. I've seen promiscuous and I've seen fast and loose, and believe me, sweetheart, you are neither.'

'But…'

'But nothing, Astra. You're twenty-two and…'

'Did I tell you that?'

'Shut up and listen.' Once she would have reared up at that. But now she was feeling a mite drained, and she feared Sayre would take his arms from around her if she got a touch stroppy. Sayre went on, 'If you were going to show any signs of being promiscuous, those signs would have appeared long before now.'

'Even if I deliberately suppressed any such tendency?'

'Astra. Think about it. You're a highly intelligent woman. Do you honestly think if you were the sort of woman you fear you are you would have been *able* to suppress it?' Tenderly he kissed her forehead, and he gave her a small shake. 'Has that dreadful fear crept its insidious way past that reasoning?'

'But…'

'What?' He pulled back to smile into her eyes. 'Tell me?' he urged.

Astra swallowed. 'What about—when you kissed me—that time…?'

'That time you kissed me back? Why wouldn't you kiss me back? You're a normal passionate woman. You may hate me at times but…' and here he grinned wickedly '…at others I'm sure you quite like me.' Astra smiled too—she had to—and it seemed that her smile was what he had been looking for because he seemed to relax a little. 'So,' he resumed, 'since you have the quite normal responses of any female, and since you were being kissed by a man you—at that time—quite liked, why wouldn't you kiss me back? You can kiss me again, if you'd care to,' he invited.

Astra stared at him, her smile suddenly gone into hiding. 'I…' was about as much as she could manage.

'Of course, you don't have to. There's no legal requirement.' He soothed any agitated thoughts she might be having.

'I didn't mean to tell you—about my mother, I mean,' Astra suddenly blurted out, her eyes fixed on his. 'Or my aunts. Not my aunt Delia, Greville's mother—she hasn't got a wayward bone in her body.'

'You weren't being disloyal,' Sayre soothed. 'In fact you wouldn't have said anything at all had I not been so hard on you,' he added. 'Ellen suffered because she bottled everything up.' He smiled encouragingly. 'Has it helped to talk about what was bothering you?'

Astra took another shaky breath. Sayre had wanted to help, had made her talk about her fears. 'If—if I kissed you—it wouldn't be promiscuous, would it?' she asked—wanting to show him just how much it had helped that he thought her a normal woman with purely a normal woman's responses.

'Take my word for it,' he answered, and to let her know that he wouldn't take the advantage even if she was sitting in her nightdress in the circle of his arms he sat perfectly still as he incited, 'I'd quite like you to kiss me, sweet Astra.'

For a moment she didn't know whether to laugh or what to do. But she looked from his eyes to his mouth, and then she knew what it was she wanted to do. She leaned forward, a shade nervously, it had to be admitted, and kissed him.

A shock went through her as their mouths touched. She pulled back sharply, looking at him, her green eyes wide, staring into the unfathomable depths of his dark eyes.

'No need to panic,' he assured her calmly.

She wasn't panicking. Without invitation she leaned forward and kissed him again. And she knew—she just knew! She stayed close, and when she felt Sayre's arms tighten around her fractionally she put her arms around him.

'Astra, I...' he murmured, and it was he who pulled back this time, almost as if to say, That was pleasant, but enough. But Astra smiled, a joyous released smile, released from that awful fear, and, with a small groan, Sayre bent and pulled her to him.

They kissed, long and lingeringly. 'Oh, Sayre,' she whispered.

'Everything all right with you?' he asked gently.

Everything had never been more all right. 'Oh, yes,' she sighed, and it didn't matter who made the first move—she was in his arms, his lips were parting her lips, and never had she been kissed, or responded to a kiss, in this way.

Astra held on to his warm, broad-shouldered body as each kiss broke and lengthened into another one. Sayre traced tender kisses down her throat and to her shoulders. She felt in seventh heaven when he pushed the wisp of lace from her shoulder and the strap of her nightdress fell down her arm.

She felt Sayre's caresses on her arm move to her lower ribcage—and finally he captured her hard-peaked, throbbing breast. No one had ever caressed her breast—the emotion Sayre aroused in her was just too much. 'Sayre!' she cried chokily.

Sayre, drawing a shaky breath, took his hand from her breast and looked into her face. 'Oh, Astra Northcott,' he murmured throatily. 'I do believe we're in danger of being carried away here.'

Astra stared at him. Yes, yes, she wanted to exultantly cry. But her throat felt too choked to say a word. She swallowed hard. 'Am I ready for that, do you think?' she answered huskily.

She thought that perhaps she was when Sayre bent his head and kissed her nightdress-covered breast where only a moment earlier his hand had been. Then he raised his head and, staring deep into her warm green eyes, 'Since you have to ask, sweet Astra,' he replied after a moment, 'I must reluctantly accept that the answer has to be—no.'

Astra looked down and didn't know at all how she felt about that. 'I'm—er—a bit mixed up,' she confessed.

'It's been quite a night,' he agreed, then smiled, and kissed her briefly. 'Goodnight,' he said—and went quickly.

Astra smiled after him. She was in love with him, of course. She could deny it no longer. Did no longer want to deny it. Why would she want to? That knowledge had brought her such tremendous relief. It was so utterly, utterly wonderful.

Both Yancie and Fennia had said that once you fell in love promiscuity and loose morals just didn't figure. Because, once in love, you wouldn't want to be in any man's arms but his.

It was true! And it was wonderful! She wanted to be in no man's arms but his. She loved Sayre, was in love with him. Loving him had released her from those terrifying fears of that family gene. Oh, wasn't life wonderful?

CHAPTER SEVEN

As MORNING came, so Astra's feeling of euphoria departed. Oh, she still experienced a massive feeling of relief to know for certain that she was nothing like her mother where men were involved. But with the coming of day that mighty feeling of release was tempered by the knowledge that, while she was in love with Sayre, he was not in love with her.

That she was in love with him was something which, at last acknowledged, would not go away. Oh, how she had buried her head in the sand about what was happening to her. This, this love, she accepted now, was the reason why Sayre had been in her head so constantly. This was the reason for her panicky feelings. Oh, how fate must have laughed when she, in her wisdom, had decided to have nothing to do with love. She hadn't had the option to decide—it was just there. She knew—she just knew. She couldn't explain it. It was just there.

There, and it was new, and she was afraid. Sayre must never know. More importantly, he must never find out how she felt about him.

She knew he could be hard and with a no-nonsense attitude, but she had also seen him good and kind—last night had shown that when he'd taken the trouble to stay and delve, to find out what the fears she had nursed for so long were all about. But, while Astra felt confident she would cope should they go into battle on some future occasion, her love for him made her vulnerable and nervous, so that should he talk to her gently, kindly, as he had last night, then she might in a soft moment be unwary enough to let him see her true feelings. And her pride wouldn't stand that.

Her eyes grew dreamy when she thought of being in his arms last night. Would she have let him make her his? On reflection, she thought, probably not. That 'marriage or nothing' pledge she and her cousins had made six years ago... While she owned she had wanted more and more of Sayre's kisses, it was an ingrained vow that wasn't so easy to overcome—unthinking though his kisses could make her.

This morning, she was glad Sayre had called a halt—if a tiny bit irked that he had so easily bade her goodnight and left. Then she remembered, with something akin to dread, how, only on Saturday night, he had told her that he saw complications ahead should he make love to a virgin. That she might be the clinging type!

Alarm bells rang loudly. Clinging! He feared she might be the clinging type! She might be in love with him—well, she jolly well was—but clinging!

Astra had her suitcase packed before breakfast. Rather than disrupt the early morning routine, she had kept to her room the previous three mornings until after Sayre had left for his office. She saw no reason to vary her habit today.

Taking care to keep out of sight when she heard his car, she looked out of the window, her insides going all weak when she saw the back of him. That she should feel so soft and all marshmallowy inside just from seeing him settled the issue. No way dared she still be at Abberley when he returned home tonight. She needed distance between them, time, space—space to get herself together.

'How's your head this morning?' Ellen enquired as soon as she saw her.

'As though I'd never had a headache,' Astra answered. While wanting to ask how the evening had gone with Greville, she was also afraid of putting any emphasis on what—though meaning a great deal to her cousin—might for Ellen have been no more than a simple dinner out. 'Actually, Ellen, when my head cleared...' oh, what a fibber she was, but it had to be done '...I remembered some important paperwork I should be attending to. You've been so good having me here,' she went on, which wasn't a lie, 'but I really feel I must get back...'

'I've enjoyed having you here—we both have,' Ellen said genuinely, and a little diffidently. 'Perhaps Greville could call at your apartment and collect the paperwork for you?' she suggested.

Oh, Greville! Oh, how could she not have thought of Greville in all of this? If she left Abberley he'd have no excuse to come down and see Ellen. Against that, though, Ellen had said both she and Sayre had enjoyed having her there—but Astra wasn't so certain about Sayre. Surely he must want his home back to himself again—she was supposed to have left on Sunday. Pride reared.

'A lot of the stuff is on my computer,' she invented. 'I really feel I should go home. I'll phone for a taxi if I...'

'You'll do no such thing,' Ellen cut in at once. 'If you really must go, I'll drive you.'

It wasn't easy to leave. Astra knew she was deliberately cutting off all chances of seeing Sayre again. But when she might have hesitated she remembered the word 'clinging', and Sayre's fear that she might be the clinging type—not that she had given herself to him—and that settled the matter.

She had been back in her apartment a couple of hours when she knew she could delay ringing Greville no longer. If she didn't call him soon he might well be driving down to Abberley on the pretext of seeing her.

Greville often had work out of his office but Astra was fortunate to find him at his desk. 'You're going to hate me,' she opened.

'I doubt that very much. What have you done?'

'I'm at home. I've left Abberley.'

'You're all right?' he asked, and added more urgently, 'You haven't fallen out with Ellen?'

'Ellen has been super. She's every bit as lovely as you think she is. She drove me back, actually.'

'Good,' he said. Then, typically Greville, he asked, 'You're not unhappy about anything, love?'

'Only that I've rather put the kibosh on your excuse to go down to Abberley.'

'Don't give it another thought,' he answered. 'I arranged last night to see Ellen on Friday.'

Astra came away from the phone mightily relieved on Greville's behalf and pleased for him that he had a date with Ellen tomorrow evening.

She spent a restless night staring at the phone as though wishing Sayre would ring. Why would he, for goodness' sake? He did not call.

Someone did ring the next day, however—her cousin Yancie. Astra remembered how she had promised Yancie to let it happen if she did fall in love. Let it happen? She had been powerless to stop it.

'So where have you been?' Yancie wanted to know. 'Both Fen and I have been wearing the wires out trying to contact you!'

'What's happening?'

'Nothing's happening. We just couldn't reach you and Greville was sounding mighty mysterious when I contacted him on Monday to ask if he knew if you'd gone away.'

'I have been away.'

'Where…? No, don't tell me. I'll come over.'

'No!' Astra exclaimed before she could give herself time to think.

'No?' Yancie queried. They'd lived with each other, knew each other's soul. 'Something's wrong. I'll come over,' she repeated.

Yancie had tenacity. Astra knew once Yancie suspected something was not quite as it should be she would work and work at it until she had the answer. 'I've—hurt my foot,' she had to confess.

Not too long later, both Yancie and Fennia—with Fennia having been collected on the way—were in the apartment cosseting their cousin. They both wanted to take her back to their homes. Astra wasn't having that.

'I'm fine,' she assured them. 'I really am.'

'I'll look in tomorrow,' Fennia said.

'So will I,' Yancie seconded.

'No, you won't, either of you. Tomorrow's Saturday and your husbands will be home. And...' she laughed '...for heaven's sake take that dreamy look off your faces, both of you.'

Her cousins rang the next day to see if she needed anything. She didn't. Greville phoned too. Sayre did not. Astra knew she was being totally illogical in even entertaining the mere whisper of a thought that he might ring to enquire how she was getting on.

Good grief, there was no reason why he would. So he had kissed her a few times, but they weren't even friends. In truth—she was pining for him.

Someone other than family did ring, though. Paul Caldwell. 'You're back home!' He sounded delighted. She had been on the way to forgetting him. She wished she could forget Sayre Baxendale as easily.

'Paul! How are you?'

'I'm fine. I wondered if you were up to having dinner with me tonight?'

She didn't date. But, hang on a minute, that was in the past. She didn't used to date when she feared she might have inherited some of her mother's less favourable tendencies. Loving Sayre had changed all that. Besides—jealousy took a little stab—it was for sure he wasn't staying home on a Saturday night.

'I'd behave myself—I promise!' Paul thought to mention when she hadn't answered.

Astra thought no further. The swelling had gone down and she could now get a shoe on her foot. 'I'd like to have dinner with you, Paul,' she accepted.

Astra got ready that evening determining that she was going to forget Sayre Baxendale. She donned a dress of warm violet and, for once, wore her hair out of its usual classic knot.

'You look positively stunning!' Paul exclaimed when she opened the door to him. 'And honestly, I'm not making a pass—I've remembered my promise—you just are.'

Astra still limped slightly and when Paul offered his arm she felt she would look less ungainly if she held on to it. He was pleasant company, and as good as his word—apart from the occasionally mildly flirtatious comment which he seemed unable to resist.

She had little appetite, so ordered something light. Paul put himself out to be amusing and Astra inserted a comment of her own here and there, and the meal passed quite companionably.

Paul was paying the bill when her eyes were drawn across the far side of the room—and her heart turned over. There, having just been directed to a table, was the man she had dined with Paul to forget. Sayre's companion was the glamorous Maxine Hallam.

Sayre was not smiling, Astra noted, her heart pounding. If anything he looked very annoyed about something. 'Sit tight, Astra,' Paul suggested. 'I'll go and rustle up a taxi— no point in your standing on that foot needlessly.' And, before she could tell him that she'd rather go with him and stand on her injured foot than sit there and have Sayre Baxendale glaring at her, Paul had gone.

She was determined not to look at Sayre again. In fact she was determined to leave—Paul couldn't be very far away. She reached for her evening purse but somehow, despite her good intentions, could not resist a flick of a glance to where Sayre was.

He had just risen to his feet, she saw. He had his back to her, but Maxine—touching his arm, of course—with a beaming parting smile, was, by the look of it, on her way to the powder room. Astra's heart picked up speed when she observed that Sayre had not resumed his seat, but, turning, was looking over to where Astra was sitting. His expression did not lighten any when he began to make his way over. Swiftly she lowered her eyes, her heart racing fit to burst.

He stopped in front of her and she had to look up. Fierce dark eyes stared back at her, and Astra guessed Sayre had something not very pleasant to say to her. Good! She could handle not very pleasant; it was gentle and kind she had trouble with.

'Why did you run away?' he charged without preamble.

Like she was going to tell him! 'You've only just discovered I'm missing?' Oh, no. Oh, heavens—that sounded every bit as if she wanted him to miss her! As if she had sat by the phone desperate for him to call her! 'I'm sorry,' she said at once, smiling. 'You were so kind to have me stay...'

'Kind!' he scorned. 'What's with the paperwork?'

Ah, she should have guessed he wouldn't swallow that one. 'I don't ask you to tell me about every project you're working on,' she answered smoothly, and could only thank her business training—and perhaps some inner inherited something from her father—that outwardly she managed to appear unflappable. 'Ah—here's my date,' she smiled, her stomach churning—Sayre would never know it. 'You remember Paul?'

'Sayre!' Paul exclaimed. 'How goes it?'

While the two men exchanged a few comments, Astra got to her feet—and found Paul there taking a proprietorial hold of her hand and tucking it into his arm. Abruptly, and without saying 'Goodnight', Sayre went back to his table.

'He's keen!' Paul commented. And, obviously observing Sayre's dinner partner who had just returned to their table, he added, 'And why wouldn't he be? He's with the delectable Maxine.'

As if sensing or having discovered that Astra was very different from his usual kind of date, Paul, true to his promise, behaved himself. As he was swift to tell her on parting.

'Have I earned the chance to take you out again?' he asked winningly.

Astra looked at him; her heart was heavy, but it wasn't his fault. 'Call me,' she invited.

He beamed, kissed her cheek, and went cheerfully on his way while Astra faced the fact that she had never felt so down. Her thoughts, she supposed, should have been on the man she had just parted from. But they were not.

Quite obviously Sayre had taken exception to her lying to his sister and that 'paperwork' excuse she had used for leaving Abberley. After such wonderful hospitality, she had to acknowledge that to lie wasn't much of a thank-you for their kindness to her. Astra realised she had no defence, other than she had never expected to extend that weekend anyhow. So, okay, she didn't have a job, but how did *he* know she *didn't* have paperwork she wanted to get on with?

Astra was up early the next morning and, with Sayre dominating her thoughts, she was glad when Fennia and then Yancie rang. She assured them she was fine and that her ankle was barely any problem now. She didn't tell them she had been out with a man called Paul, but that was because when she had been about to, all she could remember of the evening was Sayre being there.

She looked at her watch around midday and calculated it would probably be seven o'clock in the morning in Barbados. Her father was an early riser. She rang him. 'I didn't get you out of bed?'

'How dare you, young lady?' he teased. 'Who d'you think it is who wakes the birds up?'

She had a pleasant conversation with her father, during which he suggested again that now she was no longer a working woman she go over to Barbados to live. She'd love it there, he told her.

But Astra knew she wouldn't go to Barbados to live. She had already cut herself adrift from Sayre by leaving his home—not that she had ever been moored to him. But by living in London, a place where he spent his working life—and, remembering Saturday, some of his social life—and given that her cousin had spent some time, and hoped to spend more, with his sister, Astra reasoned she did at least have some small chance of bumping into Sayre on the odd occasion.

The next occasion came sooner than she could possibly have expected. She had barely put the phone down after speaking with her father than somebody rang the apartment doorbell. It must be someone that the security guard knew, she realised, otherwise he would have rung to check if her visitor was expected. Perhaps it was Greville.

She opened the door, and immediately felt warm colour rush to her cheeks—it was Sayre. 'How did you get in?' she asked, her brain witless—all she could think of was what a mess she must look: jeans, tee-shirt and no make-up, her hair pulled back in a band. She was glad to see that he was casually dressed.

'There are ways,' Sayre grunted.

He didn't sound very civil, but she considered one of them should remember their manners. Besides which, while she wasn't going to show it, she was delighted to see him. Her heart lifted; the sun had come out on her day.

'Come in,' she invited, leading the way into the elegant drawing room. She was conscious of Sayre beside her every step of the way. 'Would you like some coffee, a drink?' she asked.

'What's with you and Paul Caldwell?'

Astra blinked. 'What sort of answer's that?'

'Is he the reason you left Abberley?' Sayre gritted, not deflected one iota.

Dog with a bone again, Astra realised. 'Take a seat,' she suggested. Somehow they were standing by a sofa with a low table blocking her way. She felt he was too close, but she couldn't get by him without making an exaggerated move, and no way was she going to. No way was he going to know how being close up to him, not even touching, affected her.

'Did anything in our discussion last Wednesday trigger off your inclination to date all and sundry?' he demanded.

Astra stared at him open-mouthed. All and sundry! One date she'd had. Just one date—and that was all and sundry! Sayre had made her angry, and she was glad. She could handle angry too! 'It's early days yet,' she controlled her anger to reply sweetly.

'You weren't letting your hair down *too* much last night, I trust?'

It surprised her that he'd even noticed her hair was out of its usual knot last night, but she was even more surprised by the insinuation behind his question.

'What's it to you?' she answered icily, her control on her temper starting to fracture.

He didn't care for her tone; she could tell that from the hostile glint in his eyes. Though his tone was more silky than anything when he pleasantly told her, 'I should hate to think you were progressing too fast from where you and I left off on Wednesday.'

Astra was appalled. 'How *could* you!' she gasped, staring at him, horrified. 'How could you, after all I confided in you, accuse me of being...?' Words were not sufficient. She was going to hit him—hadn't he been asking for it long enough? But just as her hand came up so, as though already regretting what he'd just said, his hands came to her arms, preventing her from hitting him as he so richly deserved.

Frustrated beyond reason, Astra gave him a violent shove. She stumbled—he tried to steady her. But he was off balance and couldn't hold her. Her ankle twinged, and, a mixture of arms and legs, they both fell on to the sofa.

Astra was too enraged to care. 'Let me up!' she yelled when they had sorted their limbs out.

'Stay...' Sayre began, grabbing hold of her and preventing her from going anywhere. 'Listen...'

'I've heard all I want to hear from you,' she snapped, close to tears and feeling she would hate him for ever if so much as one teardrop fell.

'I didn't mean what you thought I meant.' He refused to let her go.

'Why should I care? You're leaving.'

'Come here, you daft...'

'I've had enough of your insults,' she flew, still struggling to be free.

'I wasn't so much accusing you of being promiscuous, you hot-headed she-cat,' Sayre stated, sitting up but still holding her there. 'W—'

'It sounded very much like it to me!'

'What do you think I am that I'd...?'

'How long have you got?'

His mouth twitched. Oh, she loved him so! As furious with him as she was, she still loved the swine. Her lips twitched too, and she wanted to hate him afresh because he could make her laugh while, at the same time, she wanted to knock his mouth-twitching head off.

'Believe me, Astra, I wasn't throwing anything back at you. I value your confidences about those nightmarish fears you had—even if I did have to drag those confidences out of you.' By then Astra was sitting up too and, now that she was calmer, Sayre placed an arm about her shoulders. He was half cradling her when he went on, 'I just—well, sort of got it into my head that, now you know you've got nothing to fear in the promiscuity department, you might rush too quickly to—experiment.'

'You wouldn't call that promiscuity?'

'I'd call that a healthy curiosity to—er—know what it's all about.'

Astra turned her head and looked at him. She loved him so, she didn't want to fight with him. She kissed him—and was stupefied that she had.

'I didn't mean to do that!' she exclaimed, aghast.

'I'm glad you did.'

'It's all your fault.'

'Of course.'

'You—you unnerve me. What did you come here for, anyway?'

'Now don't get narky again, or *I'll* have to kiss *you*.'

Oh, she wished he would. She looked from his eyes to his mouth, his wonderful mouth—and felt confused. 'Oh, I think you and I—um—have done—er—quite well in that—um—department already.'

'Why are you nervous of me?' he wanted to know. 'Why do I unnerve you?'

It wasn't him precisely that she was nervous of—but herself. Heaven help her, uninvited, no lead-up, no nothing, she had kissed him. So, okay, it had been more a meeting of lips, and fleeting at that, but who was to say what she would do next? This man whom she loved had the power to scramble her brain.

'I'm not so much nervous as…'

'As?'

'Did I really kiss you just now?' She could still barely believe it.

Sayre smiled. 'Like this,' he murmured, and placed his mouth over hers, a little longer than fleetingly.

'Oh!' she gasped faintly—and wanted more. She looked at him, trying to read what was in the dark depths of his eyes, but could tell nothing. What he was seeing in hers she couldn't have said, but gently his arm about her shoulders began to firm and slowly, and she wasn't resisting, Sayre pulled her close to him and she was getting her wish.

Gently at first they kissed. A slow, gentle, pleasurable kiss. He placed his other arm about her and he kissed her again, more deeply, and Astra was no longer trying to think, but feeling only. She loved him and it was a cold, starved world when she couldn't be with him.

Again and again, in unhurried but growing passion, their lips met. Sayre pressed against her and Astra pressed back. Oh, it was so wonderful that he was here. She had so ached to see him, to be with him.

His hands caressed her back and she wanted to cry out from the pure pleasure of it. She loved him; nothing else mattered. Sayre held her to him as he kissed her throat.

He released her glorious red hair from its band and buried his face in its fragrance. 'Astra, sweet, sweet Astra,' he murmured, and she unashamedly kissed him.

Then he was kissing her again, a deeper kiss than ever before, and as a need started to burn in her, out of control, she wanted more, much more.

Shyness almost tripped her up when she felt his warm, sensitive fingers on her bare skin beneath her tee-shirt. She clutched on to him as his caressing hands came to the front of her and climbed their tender way upwards.

She realised Sayre had felt her clutching movement when, 'Relax, sweet Astra, relax, my dear,' he breathed against her ear. And as his hands captured her breasts, and albeit she drew a shaky breath, it was wonderful.

So wonderful she wanted to touch him too. She risked opening one button of his shirt. 'Forward madam,' he teased, as if delighting in her—and the next she knew he had removed his shirt and she was staring at his sensational chest.

Astra stretched out a curious hand and touched one of his nipples. Then, liking the feel of that touch, she raised her head to look into Sayre's eyes. 'I want to kiss you—may I?' she whispered. 'Am I completely without shame?' she asked hurriedly as an afterthought.

'What you are is a pure delight,' Sayre replied softly.

She wanted then to tell him how much she loved him. But reserve held her back. Though how it should be that she still had reserve in some area when she quite unashamedly bent and kissed his nipples, first one and then the other, was a mystery to her.

Then nothing seemed to matter for quite some while because she was in Sayre's arms once more, passionately returning every kiss. Astra felt Sayre removing her tee-shirt; shyness battled with a desire to press her skin against his skin—and desire won.

Though she involuntarily clutched at him again when she felt his fingers busy at her bra fastening. 'Sayre, I...'

He glanced down into her flushed face. 'You're not sure?' he questioned gently.

She swallowed—oh, she wanted him so much. 'I'm sure,' she answered, and was tenderly kissed. As she held on to him so he removed her bra, and as he bent and kissed her breasts, his tongue creating havoc with first one hardened peak and then the other, Astra released a sigh of pure and utter rapture.

She knew she would deny him nothing when Sayre pulled her to him and she felt his naked chest against her nakedness—and her desire for him went spiralling out of control.

'I want you, Astra,' he groaned, tracing kisses down her throat, one hand causing yet more havoc in her desire for him when he caressed the silken skin of her left breast, moulding, teasing.

'I want you,' she cried, and was kissed long and lingeringly.

But, when she had been certain she would deny him nothing, when Sayre tenderly asked, 'Where's your bedroom?' something stirred in her that she didn't want to stir.

Sayre had said he wanted her—and she understood that. She had said she wanted him too, and that was true. But she wanted him because she loved and desired him. However, there was no mention of love in Sayre's desire. Not a word of love hammered in her brain, intruded into her brain—only a mention of his desire.

'I—er...' she gasped, trying to make sense of this belated stirring that seemed to be hell-bent on reminding her of those avowed 'marriage or nothing' years. 'I'm sorry, I really am,' she choked, pulling back from him, grabbing her tee-shirt and ramming it over her head. Sayre stared at her, stared at the thin covering over her bra-less breasts. He was still looking at her as if just not crediting this latest development, when Astra saw a muscle jerk in his temple.

'You mean—that's it?' His tone was incredulous.

Astra barely knew what she meant; how could she deny this ache inside for him? 'Y-you mentioned s-something about a healthy curiosity,' she dragged out of her memory. Oh, help her, she felt so shaky. 'I—er—think my curiosity has been sufficiently satisfied.' She took a rather desperate breath and told him because she had to, because that was the way it was, 'Sayre—I don't want an affair.' She had no need to go on; he'd got the message and was already shrugging into his shirt and buttoning it. But a sudden awful thought struck her that he might misread her declaration that she didn't want an affair with him—and think she might be hinting at marriage. 'I don't want marriage either!' she rushed to tell him.

'Good!' he replied tautly. 'While I might accommodate the one, I couldn't accommodate the other.' And, even more succinctly, he gritted, 'Marriage was never on the menu!' His glance went briefly from her face to take in the still hard peaks of her breasts which her tee-shirt could not hide. Astra saw his jaw clench, then, without another word, he strode from the apartment.

Astra was close to tears and was still inwardly trembling. She loved him, his lovemaking had been so magical—and yet there was something in her that said, This far, but no further. She could have cried at her naïveté in telling him she didn't want marriage. Why had she to mention marriage, for goodness' sake?

Well, he'd soon put her straight on that, hadn't he? 'Marriage was never on the menu!' Swine! She loved him. Pride, she supposed, had made her tell him she wasn't interested in marriage. But yet, after all those years of being certain she would never marry, or want to, Astra faced the fact ten minutes later that, having fallen in love with Sayre—not forgetting she had always been against marriage for herself—if he asked her she might well consider it.

Which just showed how truly pathetic she was, she decided as she strove to find some backbone. The phone rang; she almost didn't answer it. If it was one of her cousins again, she would have to sound bright and cheerful. Though since they had already phoned that day it wouldn't be them. Her mother?

Astra went and picked up the receiver. 'Hello?'

'Are you all right?' enquired a voice she had not expected to hear in a very long while. He who had asserted,
'Marriage isn't on the menu!' Her knees went weak.

'Never better,' she answered cheerfully; it surprised her
that she could speak at all, she was so shocked to hear him.
'Yourself?'

'The same,' he replied. A pause then, 'See you around,'
he said, and the line went dead.

'Goodbye,' Astra whispered to the air, tears streaming
down her face. 'See you around,' he'd said, and she knew
what that meant; didn't she just? As plainly as if he'd said
it, Sayre had meant exactly the opposite. 'See you around'
meant she never would—not if he saw her first.

Astra was still trying to come to terms with the only
conclusions she could possibly draw from Sayre's phone
call when her phone rang again. Again she was disinclined
to answer it. But, as the ringing persisted, Astra knew that
if it was her mother wanting to speak to her about something, then if she couldn't get an answer Imogen was just
as likely to come round to the apartment and camp on
Astra's doorstep, so determined would she be to speak to
her daughter.

Astra didn't feel like company. She went to the phone.
It wasn't her mother, it was Paul Caldwell.

'I told myself I was going to wait until Tuesday to ring
you. But…are you doing anything this afternoon?'

Astra didn't want to see anybody, and that included Paul.
She needed privacy. She had wounds to lick, and she
wanted to do it in private. 'Actually, Paul, I'm going to
Barbados to live,' she heard her voice tell him of her un-
thought plan. And liked the idea. 'I'll be spending the afternoon packing.'

Astra phoned her father—he was overjoyed. She had not
changed her mind the next morning. There was nothing to

keep her here. Oblique though his farewell had been, Sayre had said goodbye in a very definite fashion.

There was a lot to do, but a week later Astra had changed her address from her father's apartment in London to his beautiful home in Barbados.

She had not seen Sayre, or heard from him again for that matter—she had not expected to. Yancie and Fennia had at first been astonished when she'd told them of her intention to go and live with her father. Though, since they were well aware of his frequent requests for her to go and see him, they were quickly able to come to see it as quite a normal thing to do. After their initial reaction, they set about helping her pack and close up the apartment.

'What are you going to do about your car?' Yancie, never the practical one, surprisingly thought to ask.

Astra, who up until then had always been known as the practical one of the three, just hadn't given her car a thought. 'I'll sell it,' she replied. She wasn't coming back. Burn your bridges behind you—that way, should she have a moment of weakness, there'd be nothing to return for.

Astra expected a few sticky moments with her mother, then learned that Imogen was away on holiday with some man named Hedley and wouldn't be back for a couple of weeks. Astra wrote a letter and posted it to her mother's address.

Telling her aunt Delia and Greville Astra left until the last moment. Why she wanted to be gone when Sayre heard the news she couldn't have said; she just did. He might not get to hear it, she knew, but just in case Greville had started to become a frequent visitor to Abberley she left it until the day before her departure to go and see her dear aunt. From her aunt's home, she phoned Greville.

And now here she was in sunny Barbados, seemingly without a worry in the world. She had everything she could possibly want—sun, sea, a wonderful climate—and had been made more than welcome by her father. But what she didn't have was peace of mind.

Astra had been in Barbados two weeks, and felt much the same as she had when she had arrived. Sayre was in her head all of the time. When did it start to get better? Though it was through her love for him she had learned she did not possess the Jolliffe gene. Through his love-making, she had learned that she was her own person and very different from her dissolute mother.

Astra swam every day and tried to forget Sayre. But she had only to float on her back in her father's pool and in the stillness Sayre's face would appear. Sayre, who might be interested in an affair, but who had no use whatsoever for marriage. *Oh, forget him, for goodness' sake, do.*

Astra had been in Barbados a month when she faced the fact that she was never going to forget Sayre. She also accepted that since she just wasn't used to a life of idleness it might be a good idea if she found herself something to do. There were a goodly number of insurance companies on the island, management companies, bankers—perhaps she might make a career with one of them.

Her foot was no longer troublesome; what was she waiting for? For all he was retired, her father was well known in the business community, and he would know whom to approach. She went in search of him.

'Dad,' she began when she ran him to earth reading his paper. But before she could put any kind of career question to him the telephone rang.

'Saved by the bell,' he smiled, observing her serious expression, and, taking up the phone, he exclaimed, 'Greville!' After Astra had experienced a few moments' disquiet that something dreadful had befallen her aunt, she began to realise from the general tone of her father's side of the conversation that nothing diabolical had taken place. 'I expect you'd like to speak with Astra. Yes. She's here now.

Give my love to your mother. I've always had a soft spot for Delia.'

Astra took the phone he offered. 'Greville. How nice to hear you.'

'My news is even nicer!' he answered, and there was such joy in his voice that Astra knew something pretty fantastic had happened.

She smiled, happy for him. 'Would I be too far out if I guessed it had something to do with Ellen?'

'Exactly on target.'

'You're...' She hesitated. It was a bit soon, but, 'You're getting engaged?' she guessed again.

And was left open-mouthed with shock when, overjoyed, Greville announced, 'Better than that—we're getting married—on Friday.'

'Marr... *Friday!* Hang on while I find a chair.'

'Isn't it marvellous?' Greville went on euphorically, adding that although it might seem sudden to others he had never been so certain about anything. After the initial first few dates, he and Ellen had spent so much time in each other's company and had got on so well that it had become painful to part. When he'd told Ellen of his feelings and sweet Ellen had told him that she felt the same about him, it seemed a nonsense—since they were now spending every spare moment together—that he should take Ellen back to Abberley and leave her there, when she might more easily live in his home.

'And you're getting married Friday? Oh, I'm so pleased for you Greville.' Astra was absolutely delighted. He deserved every happiness.

'I knew you would be. It will only be a small affair— the wedding. Both Ellen and I had the bells, the choir, hundreds at the reception last time, and look how our marriages turned out! So this time we've decided on just Ellen and me, and two witnesses.'

'Oh, I do so wish you well!' Astra cried, so happy for him after the dreadful time he'd had when his previous marriage had fallen apart.

'You'll be coming to wish us well in person, I hope?' Greville surprised her by saying.

'You want me there? But you said you only wanted two...' No, no. The idea was unthinkable. Already, just thinking of Sayre, that Sayre would be one of the two witnesses her cousin had spoken of, and Astra's heart was thumping.

'That's right. My mother and you.'

'Not S-Sayre?' Lord, she couldn't even say his name without stammering!

'Sayre's in Japan at the moment and is so busy we haven't been able to contact him yet.'

'He doesn't know that you and Ellen are getting married!' Astra exclaimed.

'Not yet. He's here, there and everywhere, apparently, and nobody could find him when Ellen and I tried to phone him. But he knows that given half a chance I'll take care of her—we had a serious talk before he went to Japan. Which is partly why he felt he could go without taking Ellen with him.'

'You told him how you feel about Ellen before he went?'

'He'd guessed anyway. It was no surprise when I told him I intended to marry her if she'd have me. Ellen's told me since that she'd confided in Sayre that she was in love with me. So he won't be too staggered that we'll be married by the time he comes back. Though since it's his habit to ring Abberley every three or four days, he'll know some time this week what we propose to do. Say you'll come. I'd like you there. You were there more or less at the start.'

'Won't Sayre be able to fly back as soon as he knows? Ellen would by far prefer him to...'

'I shouldn't think there'll be time. And, our wedding

aside, we know he's got an overflowing workload out there.'

'And—he won't mind—that he won't be there to see Ellen married?'

'He wants only to see Ellen happy again, and she says he'll know her feelings—about having had the full works last time, but only wanting a quiet ceremony, without fuss, this time. Quite simply, Astra, we don't want to wait. So are you coming? I'm not going to let you say no.'

'Then I'd better say yes,' Astra laughed. 'And since I've only got four days to get there I'd better get my skates on.'

Her father went with her to catch her plane. 'You do intend to come back?' he asked as they said goodbye. 'I've grown to like having you around.'

'I'll be back before you know it,' she answered, giving him a hug and a kiss.

Astra found London cold after Barbados and was pleased that, apart from having the telephone disconnected, she had not cancelled the other services in the apartment. She put the central heating on as soon as she got in and, while knowing she could have gone to stay with her aunt Delia for the short while she would be in England, she didn't feel she would be very good company just then.

She would be on form on Friday, though. When Ellen told her brother about her wedding day, Sayre was going to hear only how happy and light-hearted Greville's cousin had been that day.

It was raining when Astra awoke on Friday morning. But when, dressed in a light wool suit of a most lovely turquoise-blue, Astra left the apartment the rain had stopped and the sun had come out. 'How's Sayre?' she would say casually—and happily—to Ellen, probably as the four of them sat down to lunch. *Oh, do stop thinking about him.*

Astra made a point of being early at the register office. But Greville, anxious and with eyes on the door the whole while, was there before her, as was his mother whom he'd collected on his way. They hugged and kissed and Aunt Delia expressed the opinion that Ellen would be a daughter-in-law any mother would be proud of.

Astra wanted to ask Greville if Sayre had been in touch, and how he had taken the news of the sudden marriage. In fact she wanted to ask all about Sayre. But couldn't and wouldn't and then momentarily had her mind taken from thoughts of Sayre when the door opened and Yancie and Fennia came in.

'What are you two doing here?' Greville exclaimed, a tactless question that only families were able to get away with—without offence being taken.

'You didn't think we'd let you get married without us, did you?' Yancie beamed, giving him a hug.

'Shame on you, Greville Alford!' Fennia chipped in, taking Yancie's place to give him a hug. Both girls greeted their aunt warmly. 'If Thomson hadn't mentioned to Yancie in passing that you were taking a month off to go to some honeymoon isle, and if I hadn't sweet-talked your mother into spilling the beans, you'd have done the deed with only Astra here to represent us!'

By this time both Yancie and Fennia had their arms around Astra. 'Does life of the idle rich suit you or does it not?' Yancie declared.

'You look fabulous, Astra!' Fennia exclaimed.

'Have you two looked at yourselves in the mirror this morning?' Astra asked with a laugh, and might have added how well marriage suited them, only just then the door opened and Ellen came in, followed by a tall, black-haired man—and Astra was rendered speechless!

What...? How...? Astra strove for brain power. What was Sayre doing here? Why wouldn't he be here? It was his sister's wedding day. But—he should be in Japan! Scarlet colour flooded Astra's face as a riot of emotions stormed through her at seeing him so unexpectedly. Her heart was pounding nineteen to the dozen for Sayre, his dark gaze serious, was looking straight at her. They stared at each other. She thought he was about to smile. She looked away.

Thankfully Greville had gone straight over to Sayre and Ellen and all eyes were on them. But Astra's heart was still racing when, after greeting his soon-to-be wife and her brother, Greville set about making the introductions.

Astra had nowhere got herself together when it was her turn, and Greville smiled. 'No need to introduce you to Astra, of course.'

'No need at all,' Sayre replied. 'You could say we're quite well acquainted.'

At the thought of how she'd been half naked the last time she'd seen Sayre, Astra felt warm colour flush her cheeks again, and Sayre inclined his head. 'How are you, Astra?' he enquired evenly, his eyes on the warm colour of her skin.

Oh, this was intolerable. It seemed to her as if she'd never stopped blushing since the day she had met him. 'Fine,' she answered, tilting her chin in an arrogant fashion—well, that or fall at his feet. 'I'm glad you were able to make it.'

He never had liked her arrogance, she remembered, but his tone remained even. 'Are you?' he challenged.

She gave him a half smile—and turned her attention to his sister. 'Ellen!' Astra held both hands out to her. 'You look lovely,' she said sincerely, which, wearing a deep cream shade of dress, Ellen did. 'I can't tell you how pleased I was when Greville rang with the news.'

Astra was still battling with the shock of seeing Sayre when he should have been thousands of miles away, when a clerk came and said that the registrar was ready for them.

The ceremony passed in something of a haze, and

Greville and Ellen were pronounced man and wife. Then it was time to sign the register. 'Astra?' Greville turned to ask her to sign as a second witness.

'Perhaps Sayre...' she suggested, and looked at him. As Ellen's brother, it was his place to sign.

'I'd like you to do it,' Sayre said, just that—and her legs went like jelly.

'You're sure?' She found her voice. He inclined his head; she looked away.

A table for four had been reserved at a nearby hotel for the wedding breakfast. In no time, Sayre taking charge so that nothing should bother either Ellen or Greville on this special day, the reservation had been changed to one for seven people.

Greville and Ellen were about to get into his car to go to the hotel, when belatedly Greville remembered his mother. 'Would you give my mother a lift to the hotel, Sayre?' he asked, clearly wanting to be alone with his bride.

'With pleasure,' Sayre replied, and opened the passenger door of his car for Mrs Alford. On going round to the driver's door he looked across to where the three female cousins were all dreamy-eyed about the wedding, and asked, 'You have transport, Astra?'

She refused to go red because he had addressed her and not Fennia or Yancie, though it was true he was more familiar with her than with the other two. She nearly blushed again at how familiar, but she was glad when Yancie chirped up brightly, 'Astra's without wheels. She sold her Porsche before she went to Barbados to live. But she'll come with me and Fen.'

Apparently Fennia and Yancie had arrived together in Yancie's car, and the three cousins talked non-stop until they got to the hotel. When Astra saw she was to be seated next to Sayre at the meal, she panicked and swiftly manoeuvred so that in actual fact it was Yancie who sat next to him.

Astra caught his gaze on her, but looked elsewhere and gave herself up to being light-hearted and happy, the way she had planned to be when he wasn't going to be there. How difficult light-hearted and happy was, though, now that he was here! She loved him, her heart ached for him, but he must never know.

Astra supposed she had done very well in the light-hearted and happy department because neither Fennia nor Yancie, who knew her better than anyone, suspected that she was anything but how she appeared on the surface.

Eventually the meal came to an end and Ellen and Greville, with much hugging and kissing, were saying their goodbyes and driving off. Yancie said that she and Fennia would be taking Aunt Delia home. 'You too, of course, Astra,' Yancie called.

'It's out of your way,' Astra protested. 'I'll take a taxi.'

'I'm going your way, Astra.' Sayre spoke before anyone else had a chance to. 'It would be no trouble to give you a lift.'

She hesitated, but saw that, after having protested that her address was out of Yancie's way, she couldn't very well now change her mind and tell Sayre—when he was going in her direction anyhow—that she would go with Yancie. It would be churlish in the extreme. Likewise, she couldn't very well insist on going back to the apartment the same way she'd arrived—by taxi.

Sayre was looking at her, waiting for her answer. 'Thank you,' she accepted. He smiled.

CHAPTER EIGHT

'I'M GLAD you were able to get back to see Ellen married.' Astra, seated beside Sayre as he drove along, had a ready-made 'safe' topic all there waiting.

'I was hoping not to miss getting here.'

'You're very busy at the moment—Greville mentioned when he rang me in Barbados,' she added quickly, feeling she was labouring the point but anxious that Sayre should know she hadn't been asking about him.

'Extremely,' Sayre agreed, adding slowly, 'But there are some things that are far more important than work.'

'Of course,' she replied, knowing he was referring to his sister's special day.

'How's your ankle?' He changed the subject so suddenly, she wasn't immediately with him.

'Ankle? Oh…'

'As in stile—leaping over—didn't successfully manage it.'

'Don't remind me! Fully recovered,' she answered, but didn't want this conversation getting personal. She had enough problems endeavouring not to go all soft about him without 'personal' coming into it. 'You'll be going back to Japan shortly, I expect.' She abruptly took their dialogue away from herself and memory of his involvement that day of the piggy-back home.

'It—depends,' he answered, which she thought was a bit odd. If he was so extremely busy, she'd have thought he'd have waited around only long enough to see Ellen married and then taken the next jet out.

Such thoughts went from her head when Sayre steered

168

his car into the area where her father's apartment was. This small interlude with Sayre was over and she must smile prettily, thank him nicely for the lift home, and say a friendly—no more than that—goodbye. What she must not do was to kiss him, she instructed herself sternly as without effort she recalled how she had once felt so much love for him, she had, without the slightest lead-up, astonishingly, kissed him. There had been so much kissing in greeting and parting today, it happened at weddings, but she must keep her wits about her and not give in to any more astonishing impulses of that nature.

'Oh, here we are!' she exclaimed brightly. She didn't want him to go. She could invite him in for a coffee. Don't be crass, woman! Goodbye and thank you and get out of there. 'Thank...' she began nicely as he slowed, thinking he was going to drop her off at the entrance and go on his way. But Sayre, without a word, drove past the entrance to a parking area.

Whereupon he cut the engine, took the key out of the ignition and turned to her, his dark eyes serious as he looked at her. 'Actually, Astra, I rather wanted a word with you,' he announced levelly.

His actions were not lost on her. If she had got it right, by taking the key out of the ignition Sayre was as good as saying he didn't want that word sitting here in the car, he wanted it privately up in the apartment. Danger!

'Greville will take good care of Ellen!' she burst out, only just holding panic in check.

Sayre's answer was to open the driver's door and get out and come round to open the passenger door. Astra strove to be aloof and gave him a cool smile as she got out of the car. Where, oh, where was the person she had been before Sayre Baxendale had come into her orbit? Pre-Baxendale she had been mistress of the polite set-down.

'I haven't much in the way of refreshment,' she heard

herself burbling away like an idiot as they entered the building and went towards the lifts.

'I don't expect you have,' Sayre agreed pleasantly as they stepped into the lift and he pressed the appropriate button.

'I cleared out everything before I went away,' she burbled on. 'It's hardly worthwhile re-stocking when I'll be going back again—to Barbados, I mean—in a day or two.'

The lift stopped and Astra flicked a glance at the tall, immaculately suited man waiting for her to step out. With a start she saw he looked quite bleak there for a moment. She crossed in front of him and told herself not to be so fanciful—bleak, at the thought of her going back to Barbados? Get real!

'Would you like coffee?' she enquired once they were inside the apartment. Sayre shook his head. 'Then—do take a seat,' she invited, certain he wouldn't be staying long but suddenly knowing that since this was probably going to be the last time she would see him—fat chance of bumping into him if she came back for a holiday—she wanted quite desperately to stretch out this small time with him for as long as she could. Greedy perhaps, but she loved him so much. She went and sat on one of the sofas. 'Er—Greville and Ellen,' she began again when Sayre, taking the sofa opposite, sat looking at her but said not a word.

'This isn't about Greville and Ellen.' Sayre let her know that she had been wrong in her assumption that the 'word' he wanted with her was about her cousin and his sister. 'If I didn't fully believe that Greville will only ever have Ellen's best interests at heart, I'd have been discussing it directly with him,' Sayre informed her.

'Well, that puts me in my place!' she replied haughtily, and could have thumped him when he smiled.

'At one time your arrogance might have deflected me some slight degree,' Sayre stated. 'But that would have been before I'd got to know your arrogance for the cover it is—before I got to know the warm and sensitive woman underneath.'

Astra didn't know about warm and sensitive. What she did know was that she wasn't too happy that Sayre seemed to think he had seen beneath her cover. She didn't doubt for a moment that he knew all about women and what made them tick, but she knew she'd die a thousand deaths if his 'doctorate' in women meant he'd realised that she was in love with him.

'So you say this isn't about my cousin and your sister...' Astra said, outwardly calm—my godfathers, wasn't she going to deny every smallest suspicion Sayre had of her true feelings for him.

Though that was before, watching her every reaction, Sayre replied, 'Neither is it, Astra—it's about you—and me.'

Her jaw dropped, her eyes went huge. 'You and me? Me and you?' Her head swam. Thankfully some brilliant actress she had been unacquainted with until pride roared into action just then jumped into life and answered for her coolly, 'I'm not sure I understand?'

Sayre's eyes narrowed at her cool tone. But, having wanted a word with her, and now having gained that position when the floor was his, Astra saw he was not to be put off. Though she hoped he wasn't seeing beneath her cool tone either.

'We've come a long way from that first day we met, Astra,' he commented, seeming to her to be choosing his words carefully.

But she was so desperately afraid he might have somehow guessed about how she felt—though surely he didn't intend to refer to it?—that pride demanded she should head him off.

'Oh, we certainly have,' she agreed, cool still. 'And, with

your preconceived notion that all I was interested in was a nice fat commission, regardless of who suffered—didn't we need to?'

'Did I never apologise for that?' he asked charmingly and her heart flipped over.

'Not on bended knee, you didn't,' she answered. Adding quickly, 'Not that I want you to. It was just sort of—um—aggravating at the time that anyone should think what you did about me,' she told him sniffily, feeling a trace of relief that this 'word' didn't look as if it was to be *personal* personal but merely a clearing of air, perhaps, now that their two families were kind of related.

But no sooner were her feelings of relief starting to settle than Sayre was making her wide-eyed and on edge again. 'Oh, Astra, do forgive me,' he said. 'I shouldn't have interfered; I was quite well aware of that from the start.' He took what might have been a steadying breath, had he been in any way nervous, which of course he wasn't—*Really, Astra, don't you know better than that?*—and then, to her amazement, added, 'But my PA had pointed out an expensively dressed woman getting into the driver's seat of a Porsche, looking cool and aloof—and I was instantly attracted to her.'

Astra stared at him, stunned. 'Attracted?' she questioned, her cool tone a thing of the past. 'Did you say—attracted?'

'I did,' Sayre answered carefully. 'I pooh-poohed the very idea, of course.'

'Of course you did,' she agreed, her heartbeat steadying down to a mere gallop.

'So why, when it was nothing to do with me, was I bothering to tell Veronica Edwards to bring all her father's paperwork in so I could check it out? I had far more important matters to concern myself with.'

'I thought pretty much the same,' Astra admitted.

'So why did I call you in to see me?'

'You didn't care for what you discovered.'

'I didn't care that, having seen you just once, pictures of your beautiful face kept interrupting my day.'

Oh, help. Her face kept interrupting his day! 'Did I ask you if you'd like some coffee?' she asked as her nerves started a fearful onslaught.

'No, thanks,' he refused a second time—with a slow smile. He knows I'm nervous, she realised, and determined to do better.

'You couldn't have had that,' she agreed. Thank goodness her cool tone was back. This was more like it!

'I certainly couldn't.' Astra started to grow a little anxious at all this agreeing with each other. 'But, since I make a practice of always going to the root of the matter, I decided that you'd probably got a shrieking sort of voice. So I arranged for you to come to my office—and what did I find but that you have a lovely voice, and that, close up, you're even more beautiful? And you, Astra, became more deeply entrenched in my thoughts than ever.'

She stared at him, her voice gone from cool again to coming out sounding all husky, when she said, 'I'd never have guessed.'

'You weren't supposed to. I was hardly ready to accept the effect you were having on me myself.'

'I...' She coughed—this wasn't happening! 'I had some sort of e-effect on you?'

He looked tenderly at her and she went all wishy-washy inside. 'Oh, yes, you did, Astra Northcott,' he admitted softly.

'I'd—um—I never noticed,' she stated weakly, positively wilting as she stared at him.

The corner of his mouth twitched. 'You honestly didn't gather from the many times I found you so irresistible I just had to hold and kiss you that you may have some effect on me?'

'That's not fair—you know my biological—that is to say, my first-hand biological—experience is—er—has been a trifle neglected.' He smiled; oh, grief, that dreadful urge to kiss him was there again. 'You know what I mean—you know I'm not too bright in that department.'

'You're absolutely wonderful in "that department",' Sayre assured her gently, and looking deeply into her large and giving, beautiful green eyes, he said, 'I did get it right—you do love me, Astra?'

Her breath caught; she couldn't believe she had heard him say what he had—how could he be so cruel? Abruptly she re-ossified her spine. 'You've obviously been at the dandelion and burdock again!' she erupted shortly and was on her feet. 'I'll show you out,' she told him icily, and was already on the way to the door.

She had not expected him to move so quickly. But before she had gone more than four paces Sayre was off the sofa and had a hand on her arm, staying her. 'Don't...'

'Goodbye!' she cut in, her heart racing furiously as she tried to shake off his hand. He refused to let go.

'Shh...' He tried to quiet her. 'Don't be alarmed. I'm saying this all wrong. I didn't think I would. I thought I'd got it all sorted out in my head. Forgive me, Astra. I've never been on this route before and I'm so terrified I'm going to foul it all up. M...'

Astra looked at him—and was shaken to see that he had lost some of his colour! 'Are you all right?' she asked anxiously—her head was spinning—he'd once asked her the same question.

'No, I am not all right,' Sayre replied. 'I'm very far from all right.'

'Do you need to sit down?'

He laughed. 'Oh, my love, you're wonderful.'

Astra felt a trifle miffed—she certainly wasn't happy at

being laughed at. 'You went pale,' she told him sniffily. 'I thought you might be unwell.'

Sayre considered her for a moment, and then said quietly, 'Do you think you could come and sit down with me?'

He *was* unwell! Quickly she went with him to the sofa he had vacated. Though when she was thinking in terms of going and getting him a glass of water Sayre caught her hands in his, and wouldn't let her go.

'Let me explain, let me start again,' he requested.

No way! Though—she hesitated. Sayre had said he was terrified…and, for all his colour had come back now, he had been pale, shaken, not many moments before. 'What's to explain? And can I have my hands back?'

'I love you,' he said.

'No, you don't!' she answered without thinking. He didn't—did he? He couldn't—could he? He made no move to let go of her hands as she had requested, and Astra was suddenly so stunned, as what he had just said started to penetrate, that she needed his hands to hold on to.

'I assure you I do,' Sayre stated sincerely. 'Although I tried to deny it at first—even when it was staring me in the face.'

'Oh!' she exclaimed, still too stunned to say any more.

But, having got her sitting with him on the sofa, having started off badly, Sayre seemed determined not to make a second false start. 'I knew when I didn't care for your closeness with Greville at that party—on only the second occasion I'd met you—that you were affecting me like no other woman.'

Astra looked at him, puzzled. 'How?' she asked, not at all surprised—with the way the whole of her being seemed to be in uproar—that she couldn't work it out for herself.

'I was feeling the first stirrings of jealousy,' Sayre answered openly.

'You weren't?'

He smiled. 'You're determined to oppose me all the way, aren't you?'

'Give me one good reason why I shouldn't.'

'I'm in love with you,' he answered promptly.

'You're…'

'And until I know for certain how you feel about me I shall continue to go slowly demented.'

She wanted to smile, to kiss him, to love him. But—could she believe the joyous, wonderful words he was saying to her? Astra had never felt so unsure, so vulnerable in her life. 'I—see,' she answered as evenly as she could.

Sayre kissed her cheek and she desperately needed more ossification of her spine. 'I hope you will,' he said softly. 'I hope to make you see how it was with me. How I've been jealous of your cousin, that jealousy blinding me to the fact that it was my sister he was interested in.'

Astra looked at him, unsure still. But, having had a brush with that painful monster jealousy herself, she felt for him if he truly had been jealous and found she could do no other than relent—a little.

'Greville confided his interest in Ellen, without mentioning her name, before asking me to go to that party.' Now that Greville had married Ellen, Astra felt free to be able to reveal her cousin's confidences. 'It was only on account of his feelings for Ellen, and his panic that he couldn't remember having introduced me as his cousin, that he asked me to go to the theatre that time. He knew Ellen would be there. Although…' Did Sayre truly love her? Astra began to tremble inside. He couldn't, could he? But why would he lie? What reason…?

'Although?' he prompted.

Although what? She couldn't remember. Then she could. 'Although I didn't know until we were at the theatre that you were Ellen's brother.'

Sayre smiled and then confessed, 'And I didn't know that a month after that party I would still have you on my mind.'

Astra was staggered and almost argued, You didn't, but somehow, even if she was on a see-saw of wanting to believe every word he said, yet finding it just too unbelievable, she questioned instead, 'Did you?'

'Believe me,' he urged. 'While it's true I was busily convincing myself that I didn't want to see you, and I certainly wasn't interested in making a phone call and asking you for a date, I found myself organising a weekend party at Abberley—purely for Ellen's sake, of course. So why was I so put out when I heard you wouldn't come to Abberley without a personal invitation?'

Astra smiled then for the first time since Sayre had entered the apartment. 'You wanted me there so Ellen should feel more relaxed with Greville.'

'Hogwash!' Sayre laughed. 'Fabricator that I am, I wanted you there because just to be near you made me feel good—well, most of the time.' When Astra just stared huge-eyed at him—just to be near her made him feel good!—he added, 'I didn't feel so good, though, when, first of all, I came out into the hall and saw you all over your cousin...'

'All over?'

'Well, you were hugging him. That Friday night. That first night at Abberley, you...'

'Greville had just told me that he intended to marry Ellen if he could. I was wishing him well.'

'*Now* you tell me. Then Paul Caldwell was going into action—and I was certain I was never going to invite him into my home again.'

'Oh, Sayre,' Astra said softly. He placed an arm gently over her shoulders and her heart raced. She forgot for a few moments about her own tortured jealousy. But... 'Maxine

Hallam,' she murmured—and saw a look of delight cross Sayre's features.

'You were jealous of Maxine?'

Astra was admitting nothing. Though she did concede, 'You'd said you and Maxine weren't an item, but that didn't stop you taking her out after I left Abberley.'

'You *were* jealous!' Sayre grinned. Though he sobered to tell Astra, 'I wanted to phone you, but fought the need—how dared you leave just when I was looking forward to coming home at the end of my working day and finding you there? Though, to be more precise, I hadn't wanted to leave home knowing you were there.'

'Wow!' Astra murmured on a gasp of breath. But, striving to recover, she questioned, 'So you rang Maxine instead.'

'And had to suffer Paul Caldwell sitting where I should have been sitting. I was furious that you could leave my home to go out with a man I hadn't thought you'd had any interest in.'

Astra didn't want him furious. 'I didn't leave Abberley to go out to dinner with him,' she laughed.

'Why, then?' he asked.

And she told him. She didn't mean to. But, with Sayre just sitting there watching, and waiting, she just did. 'Because I'd discovered I loved you, and...'

'Astra!' Sayre called her name, and the next she knew he was holding her close up against his heart, his arms around her. 'I thought, I hoped, I wondered, pondered. I've been in a nightmare of hope and fear.' He kissed her. 'I love you so much!' he declared—and she believed him.

For an age they sat held in each other's arms, Sayre holding her tight, releasing his hold to pull back, to look into her eyes as if wanting to reassure himself that it really was so—his suspicion and her confirmation that she loved him.

'It's true?' he questioned, seeming to want her to say so, even though there was nothing but love in her eyes for him.

'It's true,' she laughed, and had never been so happy, nor when he held her close and kissed, and kissed her.

'When?' he asked.

'When? As in, when did I know?'

'If you'd kindly answer. I've learned so much about you, least of all that there's an imp in you that has you leaping over stiles when you think that nobody's watching. I need to know everything.'

She laughed again; was this truly, fantastically wonderful, or was it not? 'You should never have been there—at that stile—I thought you'd gone to the point-to-point.'

Sayre smiled a heart-wobbling smile. 'I'd fully intended to go—until Greville told me that you weren't going.'

'You stayed behind because of me!'

Sayre kissed her, obviously loving her incredulity. 'Because of you,' he admitted. 'Though at the time I decided I was staying home only to have some space from Maxine Hallam, who appeared to be reading more into the weekend than I'd intended. So I remained behind, and was in my study when I saw you set out on your walk.'

'You saw me go?'

'And started to get so ridiculously concerned when you weren't back when I thought you should be that I came out looking for you.'

'You didn't?'

'I did. You're going to have to stop contradicting me,' he laughed, loved her, kissed her, and went on, 'I caught a glimpse of you on your way back, and was the other side of the hedge when, the stile steps more than adequate, I saw you take a run at it.' He kissed her again, and told her with delight, 'I don't think I shall ever forget that picture of Miss North Pole Northcott taking that giddy leap.' Astra had to laugh too, and Sayre just had to kiss her again. But, it seemed, he had never lost sight of his original question. 'When?' he repeated.

She loved him, so she told him, 'It started then, I think, or maybe before. I'm not sure. You irritated me from the first—I think you knew that.'

'Whatever your reaction—you noticed me?'

'How could I not? May I be a shade bold and tell you I think you're a bit—er—wonderful.'

'Don't be shy, my darling, I love it,' he said softly.

Astra kissed him and they held each other for a long while. 'When?' Sayre prompted again.

'You carried me back to the house, up to my room—that day—and nothing was ever the same again.'

'You were so sweet, innocent—still are,' he murmured tenderly, though his tone altered a little as, obviously recalling something, he asked, 'Would you mind telling me who the devil Charles Merrett is?'

'Charles…' She gaped in astonishment, and then she too recalled intimating to Sayre that she and Charles Merrett had indulged in some kissing. 'I've known Charlie all my life—he's tame and he's lovely and was quite totally safe when I felt sufficiently curious about kissing.'

'You experimented with Charlie?'

'I thought it was experimenting but, and not meaning to cause detriment to Charlie, I think kissing a water melon might come into the same category.'

'Which tells me I've no need to be jealous of Merrett?'

'Charlie's a friend. I love you.' Sayre tenderly kissed her.

'Since—when?' he asked.

'Since…it feels like for ever! You awakened feelings in me I never knew I possessed. Awakened fears in me when we first kissed that I might yet become my mother's daughter…'

'Oh, my darling. Trust me, I know you've no need to fear on that score. I…'

'I know myself,' Astra smiled. 'I knew it as soon as I faced what I had been denying for so long. That last night I was at Abberley we kissed and I accepted then what I'd been denying for an age: that I was in love with you—' the pressure of his arms about her increased '—and I knew that in my love for you I had not inherited any "man-mad" gene, because the only man I ever wanted to hold me was you.'

'Oh, my dear, dearest love,' Sayre breathed, and long minutes passed as they just held and kissed and loved and held.

Then, looking at him, adoring him, her confidence in his love growing by the minute, she asked, 'When?' and he burst out laughing.

'Oh, but you're gorgeous,' he informed her softly. Then, addressing the question in hand, he asked, 'When did *I* finally accept that which had been staring me in the face for so long?'

'Please?'

'Well, first I was having to acknowledge that you had the power—from the very beginning—to get under my skin more than any woman has ever done.'

Astra kissed him. 'I'm loving this.'

He grinned, and kissed her back. 'I should have known I was in serious trouble when I heard myself telling you that you could end up being one of my favourite people. Doubly so when, for the first time in my life, I found it extremely irksome when, that Wednesday night, I had some work I couldn't leave to come home to you and had to stay late at my office.'

'Oh, sweetheart,' Astra sighed softly.

'It wasn't "Oh, sweetheart" the next night when I came home and found you'd gone,' he replied, placing a kiss on the tip of her nose to show there were no hard feelings.

'You were angry because I'd lied to Ellen about having paperwork to do?'

'I was angry that *you* weren't *there*—where I wanted you to be. And trebly annoyed when, a couple of days later, I saw you out dining with Caldwell. How dared you have a date with someone else?'

'Er—but you did,' Astra reminded him. 'You were out with Maxine.'

'Who said love was logical? I barely slept that night, then had to go into the office on Sunday morning—and couldn't get you out of my head.'

Oh, wasn't this wonderful, all too brilliantly, brilliantly wonderful? 'You called in to see me.'

'Do I need reminding? There was I, part way to losing my head. And there were you, naked on top except for a tee-shirt—my love, I desired you like crazy—I had to go quickly, while I still could.'

'You phoned and asked if I was all right.'

'I didn't know then whether I was on my head or heels. What I did know was that your innocence had shown in so many ways in our lovemaking. I phoned—even though it was you who'd called a stop to our lovemaking—intending to reassure you that your reactions during that time were perfectly normal and that you were not, as you had always thought you might be, promiscuous. But you sounded so cheerful, carefree, not a care in the world, that I began to feel a fool for bothering to ring at all.'

'Oh, Sayre!' She was shaken that he had been so sensitive, so caring, of her. 'I was in tears after your call.'

'No! Oh, love! Oh, I'm so sorry. I never, ever want to cause you a moment of distress.'

'And I don't want you to be upset either,' Astra said quickly, in response to his genuine remorse that he had been the cause of her tears. 'So tell me, when did you know I'd left London?'

He kissed her and smiled into her eyes. 'I was determined not to contact you, of course.'

'Of course.'

'And didn't hear you'd gone to Barbados to live until the day after you'd left.'

'And you thought, Good?'

He grinned. 'Who's telling this? And I thought, Good, that'll keep me from going round to see her or trying to keep in touch with her. So I went to Japan, still thinking much the same—at least, trying to convince myself I was thinking the same.'

'Only, you weren't?'

'Only, while I was in Japan, with everything going so superbly well, no man could ask for more, I suddenly faced that it wasn't enough. Faced that I was in love with Astra Northcott, and that I wanted her.'

'Oh!' she whispered. 'Oh, Sayre.' She smiled a little tremulously at him. 'You knew then that I loved you.'

He shook his head. 'I didn't know anything of the sort. I hoped. I played back everything in my head about you. The times we'd kissed and loved—and I knew you hadn't been like that with anyone else. So, did that denote that there was something just a tiny bit special about me for you? I couldn't decide. I remembered the way you sometimes flushed scarlet—was that from embarrassment, or was it some deeper kind of emotional disturbance you were feeling?'

'You—er—went into it pretty thoroughly.'

'I had to, my darling; it was of vital importance to me. I went over again and again that Saturday night you were out with Caldwell, when in my jealous anger I demanded to know why you'd run away. You suggested I'd only just discovered you were missing, which didn't have much significance then, but while I was sifting so finely through everything in my Japanese hotel room your words seemed to play back—as if you wanted me to miss you.'

Astra just looked at him, all her love in her eyes. 'You decided that love you I must?'

'I couldn't decide. The only decision I came to while pondering if your abrupt departure to set up permanent residence in Barbados had anything to do with me—or was I just in cloud-cuckoo land?—was the decision to go and see you.'

'Ellen had managed to contact you to tell you about her and Greville getting married today, and that I was returning for the wedding?' Astra smiled. 'You decided to leave your work and come to England and go back I—' She broke off. Sayre was shaking his head.

'I didn't hear from Ellen. All I could think of was you,' he answered. And shook Astra rigid when he continued, 'I went to Barbados to see you. But you...'

'You went to *Barbados!*' Astra stared at him thunderstruck. 'You went from Japan to Barb...!'

'I love you,' he said simply. 'You were in Barbados With you was where I wanted to be. I flew to Barbados.'

'You...!' she gasped, thrilled and delighted—and stunned. 'But—but I didn't see you!'

'You'd left to come to England.'

'You saw my father?' Astra was still gasping in her astonishment.

Sayre kissed her, smiled, and confirmed, 'I saw your father. Though I'd phoned Ellen from Barbados and heard all the news, I didn't know then that you'd already left. Great, I thought; I'd get a seat on the same plane, perhaps we could talk all the way over—surely I might pick up some more wisp of a clue as to how you felt about me. But when I got to your address you'd already left.'

Astra was staring at Sayre witlessly, umpteen questions queuing up to be asked. 'How did you know where I lived?'

'It wasn't difficult,' Sayre answered—and she realised that what with her father's business contacts, not to mention the simple expedient of looking up 'Northcott' in the phone book, it probably hadn't been.

She was still stunned but starting to recover. 'My father must have told you I'd already left,' she realised. 'Why didn't he phone me here?' she asked, but, realising her brain must have been more stunned than she'd thought, immediately apologised. 'Sorry, I'm being dim-witted; the phone isn't connected. And anyhow, my father wouldn't feel any great need to contact me purely because a friend had stopped by.'

'Precisely,' Sayre smiled.

'So you flew in...'

'And could barely wait to see you, and when I did—see you—and you went scarlet...'

'You knew I was in love with you.'

'I wasn't sure. My heart started to pound at the thought you were definitely feeling something for me. Then, when we were about to sit down for the meal and you deliberately avoided sitting next to me, I knew, whether it be hate or love you felt for me, it certainly wasn't indifference.'

'You plumped for love.'

'On balance. I shut my eyes and hoped.'

'Oh, I do so love you, Sayre Baxendale,' Astra declared.

She was held firmly in his arms, when tenderly he reminded her, 'Darling Astra, you once said you neither wanted an affair nor marriage—and I said that while I could accommodate the one I couldn't accommodate the other.'

'I remember,' she said huskily, her heart racing; Sayre looked so serious.

'Well, I have to tell you, my love, that since then I've had a bit of an inversion of opinion, and I have to tell you that, today, while I could still accommodate the one I couldn't possibly accommodate the other.'

'Oh,' she said.

Sayre oh, so tenderly kissed her. 'Today, sweet Astra, I have to tell you that marriage is the *only* item on the menu.'

Astra stared at him, hardly daring to believe what her intelligence was trying to tell her. 'Wh-what—do you mean?' She desperately needed clarification.

'I mean, my love,' Sayre breathed, tenderly kissing her, 'that I couldn't possibly consider having an affair with you. That you're just going to have to marry me.' His eyes were steady, never leaving her face. 'Will you?' he asked. 'Will you marry me?'

Tears sprang to her eyes. She swallowed hard so as not to shed them. 'Oh, Sayre,' she whispered chokily, 'I'd love to marry you.'

Greville and Ellen returned from their honeymoon a day earlier than planned in order to see Astra and Sayre married. Greville and his wife were inside the church when Astra and her father arrived. Astra's two cousins, matrons of honour, were there waiting for her.

There was a small delay while Yancie and Fennia inspected the lovely bride in her gorgeous white dress. 'I can't believe it,' Fennia smiled.

'Neither can I!' Yancie sighed.

'Nor me,' Astra whispered.

'I think I'm going to cry,' Fennia declared.

'Don't you dare!' Yancie exclaimed. 'You'll set us all off.'

All three laughed, then Fennia was saying, 'Oh, Astra, you look so fantastic,' then Carleton Northcott was taking charge.

'Come along, darling. From what I've seen, Sayre will be bursting a blood vessel if he has to wait for you much longer,' he teased. Fennia and Yancie, dressed in pale lemon overlaid with antique gold, took their places behind them, and Astra and her father began their way down the aisle.

The moment Astra saw Sayre, tall, black-haired, broad-shouldered, waiting for her at the altar, she was aware of none but him. He turned a moment before she drew level with him, and she felt her heart would burst with joy at the love and admiration in his eyes.

'Hello, darling,' he murmured softly.

And they were married.

They had a brief moment in the vestry before they were joined by immediate family, and Sayre looked down at his bride. 'Oh, Astra, my dear love,' he breathed. 'You're so absolutely stunning I can hardly believe you're real. Tell me I'm not going to wake up and find this was all a wonderful dream.'

'If you're dreaming, so am I,' Astra whispered huskily, her eyes shining with emotion and happiness.

'My wife,' Sayre murmured, and tenderly kissed her.

BACHELOR DADS

An emotional new trilogy by
bestselling author

Rebecca Winters

Three dedicated bachelors meet thrills and danger
when they each fall captive to an innocent baby—
and clash mightily with three exciting women
who conquer thier restless hearts!

Look out for:

THE BILLIONAIRE AND THE BABY
(HR #3632) in December 2000

HIS VERY OWN BABY
(HR #3635) in January 2001

THE BABY DISCOVERY
(HR #3639) in February 2001

Available in December, January and February
wherever Harlequin books are sold.

HARLEQUIN®
Makes any time special.™

Visit us at www.eHarlequin.com   HRBAD

You're not going to believe this offer!

In October and November 2000, buy any two Harlequin or Silhouette books and save $10.00 off future purchases, or buy any three and save $20.00 off future purchases!

Just fill out this form and attach 2 proofs of purchase (cash register receipts) from October and November 2000 books and Harlequin will send you a coupon booklet worth a total savings of $10.00 off future purchases of Harlequin and Silhouette books in 2001. Send us 3 proofs of purchase and we will send you a coupon booklet worth a total savings of $20.00 off future purchases.

Saving money has never been this easy.

I accept your offer! Please send me a coupon booklet:

Name: _____

Address: _____ City: _____

State/Prov.: _____ Zip/Postal Code: _____

Optional Survey!

In a typical month, how many Harlequin or Silhouette books would you buy <u>new</u> at retail stores?

☐ Less than 1   ☐ 1   ☐ 2   ☐ 3 to 4   ☐ 5+

Which of the following statements best describes how you <u>buy</u> Harlequin or Silhouette books? Choose one answer only that <u>best</u> describes you.

☐ I am a regular buyer and reader
☐ I am a regular reader but buy only occasionally
☐ I only buy and read for specific times of the year, e.g. vacations
☐ I subscribe through Reader Service but also buy at retail stores
☐ I mainly borrow and buy only occasionally
☐ I am an occasional buyer and reader

Which of the following statements best describes how you <u>choose</u> the Harlequin and Silhouette series books you buy <u>new</u> at retail stores? By "series," we mean books within a particular line, such as *Harlequin PRESENTS* or *Silhouette SPECIAL EDITION*. Choose one answer only that <u>best</u> describes you.

☐ I only buy books from my favorite series
☐ I generally buy books from my favorite series but also buy
    books from other series on occasion
☐ I buy some books from my favorite series but also buy from
    many other series regularly
☐ I buy all types of books depending on my mood and what
    I find interesting and have no favorite series

Please send this form, along with your cash register receipts as proofs of purchase, to:
In the U.S.: Harlequin Books, P.O. Box 9057, Buffalo, NY 14289
In Canada: Harlequin Books, P.O. Box 622, Fort Erie, Ontario L2A 5X3
(Allow 4-6 weeks for delivery) Offer expires December 31, 2000.   PHQ4002

If you enjoyed what you just read,
then we've got an offer you can't resist!

Take 2 bestselling love stories FREE!
Plus get a FREE surprise gift!

Clip this page and mail it to Harlequin Reader Service®

IN U.S.A.	IN CANADA
3010 Walden Ave.	P.O. Box 609
P.O. Box 1867	Fort Erie, Ontario
Buffalo, N.Y. 14240-1867	L2A 5X3

YES! Please send me 2 free Harlequin Romance® novels and my free surprise gift. Then send me 6 brand-new novels every month, which I will receive months before they're available in stores. In the U.S.A., bill me at the bargain price of $2.90 plus 25¢ delivery per book and applicable sales tax, if any*. In Canada, bill me at the bargain price of $3.34 plus 25¢ delivery per book and applicable taxes**. That's the complete price and a savings of 10% off the cover prices—what a great deal! I understand that accepting the 2 free books and gift places me under no obligation ever to buy any books. I can always return a shipment and cancel at any time. Even if I never buy another book from Harlequin, the 2 free books and gift are mine to keep forever. So why not take us up on our invitation. You'll be glad you did!

186 HEN C4GY
386 HEN C4GZ

Name	(PLEASE PRINT)	
Address	Apt.#	
City	State/Prov.	Zip/Postal Code

* Terms and prices subject to change without notice. Sales tax applicable in N.Y.
** Canadian residents will be charged applicable provincial taxes and GST.
   All orders subject to approval. Offer limited to one per household.
   ® are registered trademarks of Harlequin Enterprises Limited.

HROM00_R2   ©1998 Harlequin Enterprises Limited

Romance is just one click away!

online book serials

➤ *Exclusive* to our web site, get caught up in both
  the daily and weekly online installments of new
  romance stories.

➤ Try the Writing Round Robin. Contribute a chapter
  to a story created by our members. Plus, winners
  will get prizes.

romantic travel

➤ Want to know where the best place to kiss in
  New York City is, or which restaurant in
  Los Angeles is the most romantic? Check out
  our Romantic Hot Spots for the scoop.

➤ Share your travel tips and stories with us on the
  romantic travel message boards.

romantic reading library

➤ Relax as you read our collection of Romantic
  Poetry.

➤ Take a peek at the Top 10 Most Romantic Lines!

Visit us online at

www.eHarlequin.com

on Women.com Networks

HEUT1

CELEBRATE VALENTINE'S DAY WITH HARLEQUIN®'S LATEST TITLE— *Stolen Memories*

Available in trade-size format, this collector's edition contains three full-length novels by *New York Times* bestselling authors Jayne Ann Krentz and Tess Gerritsen, along with national bestselling author Stella Cameron.

TEST OF TIME by **Jayne Ann Krentz**—
He married for the best reason.... She married for the only reason.... Did they stand a chance at making the only reason the real reason to share a lifetime?

THIEF OF HEARTS by **Tess Gerritsen**—
Their distrust of each other was only as strong as their desire. And Jordan began to fear that Diana was more than just a thief of hearts.

MOONTIDE by **Stella Cameron**—
For Andrew, Greer's return is a miracle. It had broken his heart to let her go. Now fate has brought them back together. And he won't lose her again...

Make this Valentine's Day one to remember!

Look for this exciting collector's edition
on sale January 2001 at your favorite retail outlet.

HARLEQUIN®
Makes any time special ™

Visit us at www.eHarlequin.com

PHSM